Red Rock Ranch
Lucy's Chance

Red Rock Ranch ~ Book 1

BRITTNEY JOY

D1510730

"All horses deserve, at least once in their lives, to be loved by a little girl."

--Unknown Author

ONE

IT WAS FOUR minutes past noon and I was chasing a two hundred pound steer down the barn aisle. At three minutes past the hour I had my butt planted on the long wooden bench in the tack room and was halfway through my turkey-mayo sandwich. My first swig of Dr. Pepper fizzled down my throat and I closed my eyes, reveling in the cold, wet gulp. The cool air in the tack room reeked of worn leather and dirt.

Amidst my gulping, I'm not sure which came first: the frustrated hollers from Marilynn or a chocolate-brown blaze of fur and hooves flying past the open door. Either way, I dropped my pop can and scrambled out into the barn aisle, looking from one end to the other. Marilynn stood with her hands on her hips in the barn doorway. Her five foot, petite frame didn't make much of a silhouette against the sun, but her voice made up for it. She pointed at the steer trotting down the aisle. "Get that little bugger," she yelled, and I turned, racing straight for him.

I ran like I knew what I was doing, but I didn't. I pumped my arms and tried to lengthen my stride, but cowboy boots do not make great running shoes. Their slick leather soles slid against the concrete floor instead of gripping it. Trying not to twist an ankle, I steadied my long legs into a safer speed, but the steer didn't slow a bit. In fact, he picked up his pace. With his tail flagged high over his back, his hooves clipped against the floor as he darted out the opposite end of the barn.

Marilynn had spent the morning showing me the ropes. Mucking stalls, grooming horses, packing hay bales around—those were all going to be part of my job. I didn't recall her saying anything about tackling cattle, but I didn't want to let her down. Not on my first day. So I ran.

I burst out into the sunshine and gained speed on the gravel road leading to the pastures. The weathered fencing ahead stretched out for miles, dotted with horses and cattle, and the steer had already stopped, grazing on the lush grass like he was supposed to be there. A few of the ranch horses poked their heads over the fence, extending their necks out to sniff the visitor, and I slowed to a jog as I approached him. He picked up his head and stopped chewing, looking straight through me. "Easy, buddy," I said through heavy breaths. I raised my arms as I stepped closer, showing him that he needed to stay put.

In all the years I had worked with horses, I had never been around cattle. I assumed they were similar to horses. They were about the same size and they had the same gentle brown eyes. I would have called the animal in front of me a cow, but I was informed earlier that day that he was actually "a steer." And, *the steer* in front of me had long black eyelashes and a baby pink nose. His brown coat looked slick as silk and I felt the need to touch his big floppy ears. He reminded me of our neighbor's golden retriever, Bart, who wandered over to our house whenever I was outside, wiggling his whole body in happiness. Seeing no immediate threat, I dropped my arms to my sides and headed straight for the steer's shoulders. I didn't have a halter, but I could put my hand under his throat latch and lead him back, just like I would with a horse.

Wrong. Very wrong.

He was standing there, so sweet and quiet, like a little puppy waiting to have his head scratched. I didn't expect him to lurch forward like a shot cannon. And, upon this rash reaction, in instinct I jumped in front of him, trying to stop him from running past me. This brilliant idea only gave him nowhere to go but up. I watched it happen in slow motion and couldn't do a thing about it. In a split second, two hundred solid pounds lifted off the ground in an attempt to jump over my head. I don't know where that cow wanted to go, but he made it very clear that I was not going to be giving him any directions.

A month ago, I squealed like a cut pig when I got the job. I hung up the phone after talking to Mr. Owens, the ranch's owner, and jumped around the kitchen for fifteen minutes. I would be spending my freshman summer as a stable hand at the Red Rock Ranch. What could be better? Now, I heard a different type of squeal and I was certain it was also coming out of my mouth. I threw my arms in front of my face and just had time to brace myself for the hit. The steer didn't quite make it over my head. Instead, his chest slammed into my shoulder, spun me around, and put me face first into the grass.

Lucky for me, all four of his hooves missed my body as they found the ground. I picked my head up, thankful I didn't get stomped, and watched the steer run off along the fence line, holding his head high in the air flaunting his escape. Mental note: Cows are not like horses. Do not let the big brown eyes fool you.

Then, I watched the brown steer trot straight towards a boy with a bucket in his hand. The boy shook the bucket as he opened the pasture gate and that dang steer trotted in right after him, following the sound of grain rattling against metal. He didn't give that kid any lip or try to knock off his head. The boy overturned the bucket and grain piled onto the ground. The steer dug his nose right into the trap, licking up the goodness, and the boy walked away, untouched, shutting the gate behind him. I rested my cheek on the grass, trying to make my head stop spinning. Maybe cows *were* more like horses than I thought.

Marilynn's boots crunched through the lawn as she jogged over and then stood, looking down at me. "I didn't mean you had to wrestle with the steer." She shook her head and tried, unsuccessfully, to hold back a grin. "They don't usually take kindly to that."

I rolled over onto my back. "I'll remember that for next time."

To further emphasize my over-dramatic attempt at catching a cow, a second body came into my vision. "A little grain in a bucket is usually enough to get their attention," the ball-capped cow-whisperer noted with a wink. "You must be the new girl."

Marilynn assisted with the introduction when she realized I wasn't going to respond. "Lucy Rose, this is Casey. He's the other stable hand."

I stared at their faces, assessing the situation. It was my first day at work and I had been football-tackled by a mere baby cow. I was now lying on the ground, surrounded by my two co-workers. I probably had dirt on my face and grass stains on my shirt. I reached out my hand. "Hi, I'm Lucy. Nice to meet you."

With ten minutes before I had to be out the door, I scrambled for something to wear to the ranch sorting. Rummaging through every piece of clothing in my suitcase, I tried on five different shirts. I found something wrong with each of them.

Ignoring the mess of clothing scattered across my bed, I pulled a long sleeve t-shirt over my head and stared at the purple cotton top in the full length mirror hung from the wall. A leggy, skinny girl stared back. I turned sixteen three weeks ago, but my body seemed resistant to catch up to my age.

And what was my hair doing? The stick-straight, mousy brown strands hung on my head, brushing the middle of my back. I poked at them with a comb trying to muster up some volume. Sigh. *I guess a pony tail will work.* At least I had all the dirt smudges washed off my face and blades of grass plucked from my hair.

Looping an elastic around my hair, I looked away from the mirror and examined my home for the summer. The one-room bunkhouse had a twin bed tucked in the corner, a small oak nightstand, and a matching three-drawer dresser with brass knobs. A single light hung from the center of the A-frame ceiling. It was simple and perfect.

The employee bunkhouses were a quick walk from the ranch's outdoor arena, but the clock on my nightstand was blinking at six-fifty-four. I only had six minutes to get there. Yanking on my trusty tan cowboy boots, I hopped out the screen door, hustling down the three stairs to the dirt path. Pointed towards the arena, I examined the neat row of bunkhouses as I passed by. There were at least ten and they reminded me of a village of miniature log cabins. I wondered which one was Marilynn's. Which one was Casey's? Right now, they appeared dark, deserted.

Farther ahead, the big fluorescent arena lights buzzed as they warmed up and, beneath them, swarms of people gathered on and around the bleachers. It became obvious *everyone* was at the ranch sorting. Crossing my arms, I approached the mob of people and scanned the bleachers for Marilynn. There was quite a variety of people in the audience, but the ranch guests were easy to pick out. Scattered throughout the crowd were families and couples outfitted in GAP jeans and shiny new cowboy boots. Cameras hung from their necks and visors sat perched on their heads. Their kids danced around in plastic cowboy hats and yelled things like "yehaw" and "giddy-up."

The regulars also stuck out, sporting worn-in wranglers and real cowboy hats. Belt buckles shined from their waists. They chatted and joked together, hanging in a tight circle by the edge of the arena. A few of the girls were balanced up on the fence, eyeing the cowboys warming up their horses. They looked like they put a little more effort into getting dressed for the occasion.

I slowed to a stop on the outskirts of the crowd, feeling like an intruder. Marilynn did say to meet at seven o'clock, didn't she?

As though she heard my internal screams for help, Marilynn came into view. Clean, crisp jeans and a hint of lip gloss. "Hey!" Marilynn waved from inside the arena. "Over here!"

I rushed to her side with a few curious looks from the crowd of regulars.

"You ready for your first ranch sorting?" Marilynn asked as she pushed her mahogany hair behind her ear. The blunt ends brushed the top of her starched collar. I nodded. "You're going to be my assistant at the gate, okay?"

I grew up around horses, but had never participated in a ranch sorting. I wasn't quite sure what it was. I assumed it had something to do with the ranch...and sorting?

"Sure, what would you like me to do?"

Clipboard in hand, Marilynn instructed, "I'm going to round up the competitors in the arena and send them over to the cattle pen as the announcer calls out their names. You stand by the cattle pen gate and let them in and out. You are the official gate girl."

The official gate girl. *Okay, not the most impressive title, but I'll take it. That will put me close to the action and away from the crowd.* "I think I can do that."

Just then the Star Spangled Banner crackled over the loud speakers and a single horse and rider loped through the gate at the far end of the arena. The crowd grew quiet and stood at attention, hats off and hands placed over their hearts.

American flag in hand, the rider's perfectly curled blonde hair bounced with each stride as she rode around the edge of the arena. Her horse's chestnut coat gleamed like a new penny and its flaxen mane and tail almost matched the color of the rider's own golden curls. Her blouse glittered with crystals and her tan leather chaps were the same color as her cowboy hat. She looked like a Barbie doll.

"Who is that?" I whispered to Marilynn without taking my eyes off the rider.

"Taylor," Marilynn paused. "Taylor Johnson. Rodeo queen extraordinaire."

I digested Marilynn's statement. I couldn't tell if she was being sarcastic or matter-of-fact.

"She's really pretty," I said, also admiring her stunning horse.

"That she is," Marilynn noted. "Taylor and her mom are regulars here at the ranch. They've spent the last few summers here as guests."

Taylor didn't look like the rest of the guests in the audience. She looked like she grew up on the back of a horse...or came from the pages of Seventeen Magazine. One or the other.

"Her family has money. They rent out one of the guest houses for the summer and Taylor always brings her horse, Star."

"Oh." I scanned Marilynn's face noting her unimpressed facial expression.

Taylor guided her horse to the middle of the arena for the end of the Star Spangled Banner. The crowd clapped and the announcer thanked her as she trotted Star towards the back gate, waving and flashing her smile to all the cowboys on the way out.

"Okay, now we can get this show started," Marilynn said as she left to locate the first team of riders.

I moved to my position at the cattle pen gate, wondering how long Taylor had been working with Star. They made such a pretty picture together.

Lost in thought, I jumped when the announcer's voice boomed over the loud speaker. "Welcome to Red Rock Ranch's first ranch sorting of the summer!" His voice thundered and the crowd cheered. "Our first team is ready to enter the pen. Let's make some noise and see how fast they can round up those steers!"

That's my cue. I opened the gate plenty wide for two riders and looked up just as they trotted through.

"Watch out for those steers, Ms. Lucy." The sarcasm laced in the rider's voice was too familiar. "They can be a bit tricky."

Casey. He shot a smirk my direction as he rode through the gate. *Funny guy. Funny guy.*

"Cowboys and cowgirls, let's welcome a few local cowboys, Casey Parker and Austin Jones! Representing the town of Three Rivers!"

Locking the gate in place, I peered through the metal bars at the two riders, recognizing Casey's dapple gray horse. The big gray gelding dominated the field this morning while Marilynn and I fed the ranch horses. I scooped oats into buckets hanging along the fence line and the gray gelding was the first to dig in. He pinned his ears flat against his neck as he ate, showing the other horses who was boss. Not one horse dared to mess with him. But now, his ears were forward and pricked. He stood still and glared at the herd of cattle on the other side of the circular pen.

Then Casey leaned forward and the gray horse sauntered towards the herd. The pair stepped into the herd of ten, creating a barrier between the herd and a single black steer, marked on his rump with a spray-painted number one. The steer spun and tried to run back towards the others, but Casey and the gray shot forward to cut him off. Then, loping close behind the steer, they followed him along the edge of the pen and through the opening to a second circular pen.

Casey and his partner were a blur, taking turns to separate each steer from the herd and move them into the second pen. The horses hopped and weaved, chasing the steers in numerical order according to the spray-painted numbers on their rumps. While one rider was chasing a steer, the other rider blocked the rest of the herd from a premature entrance into the second pen. The object of the event soon became clear to me. That's why they call it "sorting."

The gray gelding seemed to listen to every quiet movement of Casey's body. They communicated with a language that no one else could hear, but I was certain it wasn't sarcastic. Casey and the gray worked together as a seamless team.

Before I knew it, the two riders had worked their way through the numbered herd and the crowd jumped to their feet as Casey chased the last steer into the second pen. The clock stopped at thirty-one seconds.

"What a way to start off the summer!" the announcer shouted and the crowd roared. Casey headed back towards me and I opened the gate. He tipped his hat at me as the big gray trotted by, barely winded, and I watched as they maneuvered out into the arena, greeted with high-fives and hoots from the other riders. That was obviously not his first ranch sorting.

As the night went on, I opened and closed the gate for another thirty pairs of riders. I watched each sorting with intensity. Although, it seemed like no one could match up to Casey and his partner's time. The closest were two sisters on matching palominos who managed to hit forty-two seconds.

The metal latch rattled as I closed the gate after the last pair of riders trotted out into the arena.

"Nice job, gate girl," Marilynn said as she came up behind me.

"Thanks," I grinned. "That was fun to watch."

"It's even better when you're in the saddle. You should give it a try. You could always use one of the ranch horses."

My body shuddered when I thought about riding in front of a crowd like that. I took a breath to respond but got distracted as I glanced over Marilynn's shoulder. Next to the arena bleachers, Casey was talking and smiling with Taylor, the blonde rodeo queen. She reached out and touched his arm, laughing at something he said that must have been hilarious and brilliant.

Marilynn caught my line of sight and turned to see what I was staring at. She wrinkled up her nose. "Wow, that didn't take her long to hunt down Casey."

Hunt down? It didn't look like he was in distress.

"Figures. Taylor tends to like the spotlight." Marilynn shrugged. "And she also seems to be attracted to guys in the spotlight. Last summer it was Justin, but only after he won the bull-riding title at the St. Paul Rodeo. Appears she's got her eye on Casey this year."

It did look that way.

"Anyhow, I'll see you in the morning," Marilynn said as she turned to leave, clipboard still in hand. "After chores, I'll need your help with a ride into Mount Hood."

My eyes snapped back to Marilynn and I forgot all about Casey and the rodeo princess. My first trail ride into the mountain? "I'll be there bright and early!"

TWO

I ACTUALLY BEAT Marilynn to the barn the next morning. The air was crisp before the sun came up and I zipped up my canvas Carhartt vest. My leather work gloves were stuffed in my pockets along with a pocket knife and a granola bar. I was ready for whatever Marilynn needed me to do today.

A few horses gave a soft nicker as I flicked on the barn lights, illuminating the aisle. My boots clicked along the floor and, one right after the other, the horses poked their heads over their stall doors. Their sleepy eyes blinked at the bright lights.

About halfway down the aisle, I recognized the chestnut with the flaxen mane and tail, Taylor's horse Star. The wide blaze on her delicate head was chalk-white and her forelock lay in a neat braid. Her ears pointed forward and she watched me as I came towards her. I reached out to rub her pretty face when, without notice, her ears pinned flat against her neck and a flash of teeth grabbed for my arm.

Jumping back, I yanked my arm away and stood, stunned, a safe distance from the stall door. I couldn't believe how the pretty mare looked so ugly with her ears still flattened, moving her body from side to side over the half door.

"She's a cranky one, isn't she?" Marilynn had just entered through the barn door with a thermos of something hot in her hands. "Very punctual, I see. That's good."

"Yeah," I said, keeping my eyes on Star. "I was up around five this morning. Had a little trouble sleeping."

"She was like that when she came here last summer too," Marilynn noted, pointing her thermos in Star's direction. "Taylor spends a lot of time trailering to rodeos and rodeo queen competitions. Star spends a lot of time in trailers and stalls and, when she's not doing that, Taylor has her in full time professional training. I'm not really sure she remembers how to be a horse."

At once I felt bad for the little mare that almost took a chunk out of my arm.

"She got better over the summer last year. She gets pasture time with us and Taylor tags along on some trail rides every now and then. Star gets a break here."

"Seems she needs it."

"She does," Marilynn agreed. "Ready to feed all these hungry ponies?"

"Sure am," I answered, grabbing a grain bucket in each hand.

The ponies were fed, their stalls cleaned, and the barn aisle swept. It felt good to push a wheelbarrow and throw bales of hay, but it would feel even better to swing up into a saddle and head out into the mountain.

I shed my vest when the morning warmed up and it looked like the sun was around to stay. *Blue skies and sunshine. What a gorgeous day for a ride. How could it get any better?*

Outside the barn, Marilynn brushed hay bits off her jeans. "Change of plans. It looks like I'm not going on that trail ride after all."

The smile dropped from my face.

"Mr. Owens has some friends staying at the ranch and he asked me to give their little boy a roping lesson this morning." She shrugged.

I tried not to let my disappointment show. "That's okay. Is there anything you need me to do in the barn while you are giving the lesson?"

"Yeah, you can help Casey tack up the horses. You're still going on the ride. Casey will lead it," Marilynn stated. "He's rounding up the horses now."

Following Marilynn's new instructions, I hurried to the horse pasture to find Casey, eager to show him I knew my way around a horse much better than a cow.

Casey already had five horses tied up along the pasture fence and was cinching up the big gray gelding he rode last night. The horses looked content basking in the morning sun and swishing at a fly here and there.

Casey had his back to me, but the gravel crunching under my boots gave me away. "You sure you don't want to tackle a steer or two before we head out?" he said, turning his head to face me. His mouth curled up in a grin.

"No, I got that out of my system yesterday," I said, narrowing my eyes at him. *I wish he'd forget about that already.*

Casey just chuckled and picked up a second saddle from the ground. "Who would you like to ride today? You point to the horse and I'll throw a saddle up for you. Every one of these steeds will treat you well."

The horses seemed to know they were being scrutinized as they turned their heads to see what we were blabbing about.

"The little palomino on the end looks sweet."

"She is," Casey replied as he went over and threw the pad and saddle on the palomino's back. "This is Sunny."

I watched Casey pull the cinch under her belly and wrap the saddle's leather latigo through the metal loop. The sleeves of his black-and-red flannel were rolled up to his elbows and he brushed his sandy hair from his eyes with his forearm. "I think I'm supposed to be helping you tack them up," I said and immediately realized I sounded ungrateful for his kindness. "Marilynn said," I added.

"If you insist." Casey nodded to the stack of saddles and bridles. "Everything is labeled with the horses' names. Next to Sunny are Jack, Freckles, and the sorrel pony is Sharkie."

I studied the tiny sorrel pony with the hay belly and raised an eyebrow. His back wasn't much higher than my waist and his frizzy, thick mane stuck out in every direction. He resembled a cartoon character.

"Sharkie?" I asked.

"Don't let his cute face fool you. He's a spitfire out in the pasture. He takes on horses twice his size. Marches around out there like he's king," Casey said, shaking his head. "But he's a teddy bear for kids."

"He looks more like a 'Sweetie' to me," I said, walking to the pile of tack. I threw a baby blue saddle pad on Sharkie's short back and scooped up a tiny brown leather saddle.

"Who's that?" I asked, nodding my head towards the big gray gelding.

"This is my horse, Rocky." Casey ran a slow hand over the gray's muscled rump. "His mom, Babe, was a ranch horse, but she colicked when Rocky was only a month old. I bottle-fed him and Mr. Owens said he was mine after that. That was five years ago."

"You two made quite the team in the ranch sorting last night."

"Thanks. He's a good boy. Takes care of me."

Casey patted Rocky, quiet and lost in a thought. It was obvious how much he cared for the big gelding.

"You headed out for a ride?" The new voice came out of nowhere and her question broke my stare. Taylor strutted right by Sharkie's tail, focused on Casey. She didn't seem to notice I was standing there, a few feet away.

"Taylor," Casey said, standing at attention. "Yes, taking some guests on a ride in about fifteen minutes. Care to join us?"

Taylor's jean shorts just covered her butt and I wondered if she cut them that short or if she in fact bought them like that. Not proper riding attire. But she did have her cowboy boots on.

"I would, but I'm supposed to have brunch with my mom and Mr. Owens. Can I take a rain check?" Taylor cocked her head and played with the end of her perfectly messy side braid, twisting the ends through her fingers.

"Sure," Casey said, clearing his throat. "Lucy and I have rides scheduled all week. Pick your day."

Her nose wrinkled at my name and Casey's eyes shifted from Taylor to me.

"Taylor, have you met Lucy?"

A sense of panic shot through me, as though I wasn't supposed to be there. Taylor turned and I

19

became aware that I probably had hay pieces stuck in my hair and manure on my hands. I wished I was saddling up one of the regular-sized horses so I could just duck and hide behind them.

"Hi, I'm Lucy." I wiggled my fingertips at her.

"You must be the new help," Taylor said flashing a forced Hollywood smile.

Interesting way to put it.

"I'm the new stablehand," I corrected her. "Here for the summer."

Taylor turned her attention back to Casey. "Casey, here, doesn't need much help," she cooed. "He's quite the cowboy."

Now I knew I definitely wasn't supposed to be there.

"Maybe I'll run into you later, Casey. Going to the bonfire?"

"I think so," Casey said, his cheeks a shade of pink.

"You should." Taylor winked.

As Taylor sashayed away, I caught Casey's gaze lingering on her departure. Her hourglass figure was accented further by the turquoise beaded belt wrapped around the waist of a tight t-shirt.

An impatient Sharkie started pawing at the ground and the sound broke Casey's trance. He looked back at me and then diverted his eyes to the ground. "You want to saddle Freckles and I'll get Jack? The guests should be here any minute," he said, walking towards the saddles.

"No problem." I wondered if Taylor had that effect on every guy she came into contact with.

THREE

THERE WAS NOTHING better than the back of a horse. The rhythmic swaying in the saddle never failed to sooth me. I rubbed Sunny's neck with my free hand and ran my fingers through her cream-colored mane. She was a sweet, quiet mare. Reminded me of my horse, Stella, at home.

Casey was leading the trail ride, followed by Freckles and Jack carrying Lisa and Steve, a California couple on vacation with their son, Simon. Simon was ten years old and couldn't wait to gallop. I'm not sure he knew what a gallop was, but that's what he told me in the first thirty seconds of meeting him.

"I feel like a real cowboy!" Simon exclaimed to me over his shoulder and then proceeded to drop his reins and circle his hand in the air, twirling an imaginary rope. Sharkie just kept moving along. The squirmy little boy didn't bother him in the least.

"Real cowboys have to hold onto their reins," I reminded him.

"Oh, yeah. I forgot." Simon grabbed the reins resting on Sharkie's neck.

The air tasted cleaner in the mountain. We had only been riding for twenty minutes or so, but we were in the thick of Mount Hood. Trees rose a few hundred feet above our heads and created a green canopy, letting only a few rays of sunlight though. The ground was covered by ferns; moss worked its way over roots and up the base of trees. And we rode single file following a well-worn path through it all. I could do this all day long.

"How old were you when you started riding?" Simon asked, pulling his straw cowboy hat off his head to examine it, but still keeping one hand on the reins.

"I was about your age," I said, thinking about all the days I spent on Stella's back. I would run out to the barn at the first sign of daylight and ride and brush and love on Stella until Dad made me come in for dinner. And then I'd spend the evening telling Dad all of my horsie adventures.

"I want a pony." Simon interrupted my thoughts. "But Mom said they don't allow ponies in the city so I got a cat instead. His name is Bob and he's orange and really hairy."

I chuckled. "Cats are nice too."

"Yeah, Bob is a nice cat. He sleeps with me every

night. He likes to sleep on my head sometimes," Simon said as he pushed his cowboy hat back on. "Whoa! I think I see a cow!"

Looking past Simon, I could see Casey and Rocky walking through a bright opening and out of the dense trees.

"Let's catch up. You want to trot, Simon?"

A squeal came out of the little boy's mouth and he nodded his head as fast as he could. I gave Sunny a gentle squeeze with my calves and we jogged up next to Sharkie. Sharkie followed and broke into a choppy, quick trot to keep up. Side by side, Simon and I trotted out of the forest. The rest of our group was waiting for us on the edge of a huge emerald field dotted with hundreds of cow and calf pairs. The snowcapped tip of Mount Hood hovered above us.

I slowed Sunny to a stop next to Casey and Simon trotted Sharkie over to his parents to tell them how much he loved the little brown pony.

I couldn't take my eyes off the scene sprawled out in front of me. "This looks like a postcard."

Brown and white cows and calves grazed on the abundance of grass. Many were laying in the sunshine chewing their cud. Their fat bellies spilled over on the ground and they paid no attention to the new visitors.

"Do all of these cattle belong to the Red Rock Ranch?" I asked.

"Yeah, there's about three hundred head total. We push them up to these higher pastures during the summer to graze. I ride up here a few times a week just to check on the herd," Casey said, relaxed in the saddle and scanning the field. "I always bring my rope just in case there's a sick or injured animal."

Movie scenes from John Wayne's westerns flashed through my head. "You rope and treat them by yourself?"

"Not by myself," Casey noted. "Rocky is always with me."

And there wasn't a drop of sarcasm in his voice. In fact, he said it like it was no big deal. Speechless, I gawked at Casey, realizing I could probably learn a thing or two from this cowboy.

Unaware of my stares, Casey watched Simon laugh and trot circles around his parents. "We better get going. Let's take these guys for a trot through the field and then head back down the mountain," Casey said, nudging Rocky forward.

I waited for Lisa, Steve, and Simon to follow and then Sunny and I fell into step. I wished Casey and I had more time to talk. I had a thousand questions for him about the ranch, the horses, the mountain. Instead, we walked in a line along the edge of the field, next to the giant fir trees. The tall grass brushed Sharkie's chest and he bit off the tips of the wispy blades as he walked.

"Silly pony." Simon giggled and patted Sharkie on the rump.

As Casey turned to ride out through the field,

something jostled in the trees. In a split second, twigs snapped, branches cracked and I realized something big was bulldozing its way through the brush, straight for us.

Sunny jumped sideways and trampled through the field backwards, moving away from whatever monster was lurking in the woods. "Whoa, girl. Easy..." I grabbed the saddle horn and tried to sound calm. Bringing her to an unwilling stop, I glanced up. All five horses were now facing the rattling brush.

Sunny's ears were so far forward that the tips were almost touching. Was the bull out in this pasture too? Would a bear attack a group of horses in the middle of the day? Scenarios traced through my head.

But, before anyone could react further, a big black figure burst through the bushes, screaming at the top of its lungs. The wild-eyed beast stopped abruptly in front of us and it took me a second to realize...it was a horse.

The second scream came from Simon and I turned to see pure fear rush over the little boy's face. He dropped his reins and wrapped his body around the saddle horn. In the same instance, Sharkie pinned his tiny ears flat against his curled neck and reared up, striking out at the foreign animal.

This display prompted the black horse to lurch forward, teeth first, at the tiny pony and screaming boy.

My instincts kicked in. Leaning forward, I kicked

Sunny into a lope. Two swift strides and I had Sharkie's reins in my hand. Without pausing, I spun Sunny away from the black horse and we pulled the reluctant pony with us, ending up behind a stunned Jack & Freckles.

Not sure what to do next, I looked back towards Casey for help and caught the tail end of a rope soaring through the air. The loop slid around the black horse's neck and Casey wrapped the opposite end of the rope around his saddle horn. He braced his feet in the stirrups, ready for a wild reaction.

Rocky backed until the rope slammed tight around the wild horse's neck, causing a series of violent bucks and rears. I watched, frozen in disbelief, as the horse flailed his body through the air. His front legs lashed out at the rope as though he was trying to pick a fight with it.

Pulling back against the uproar, Rocky dug his hooves into the ground, using all of his body weight.

Realizing he was trapped, the black horse stood still, glaring at us. His nostrils flared, taking in our scent. His sides heaved from the fight, but he was not giving up. He was ready to fight again at any prompting.

Simon was crying by this time. His mom was off her horse and holding the boy.

"What the heck?" I gasped. It was the only thing I could think to say.

Casey caught my eye and then assessed the guests.

His shoulders relaxed a bit when he realized no one was hurt and he nudged Rocky forward one step, giving the black horse a little slack in the rope.

"You just roped a mustang," I said, staring at Casey. In pictures, mustangs exuded freedom and beauty, but I had never been close to one. We were on his territory and he obviously didn't like it.

Casey shook his head. "He's not wild."

Did he just miss the part where that horse charged through the trees and then proceeded to attack us? "What are you talking about?" I shrieked.

But, in the midst of second-guessing Casey's eye sight, I noticed a thin strap of leather hanging loosely around the black horse's neck. It looked like a worn dog collar and a number plastic tag hung from the buckle. Number thirteen. Everything about this horse screamed bad luck.

"Everybody okay over there?" Casey asked as Simon's crying turned into a quiet whimper. My heart ached for the little boy who was so excited for his first horse ride just a few minutes ago. Now he probably just wanted to go back to the city and snuggle with his fat cat, Bob.

"We're fine," Lisa responded, rubbing the boy's back and then setting him on the ground. "A little shook up, but fine."

Unsettled by the crying, Sharkie turned his head and nudged Simon, rubbing his whiskered nose on the boy's arm.

"Do you know what Sharkie just did?" I asked and Simon looked up at me, confused and blinking away tears. "Sharkie was just trying to protect you. He didn't mean to scare you."

Simon was quiet, thinking about my words. He craned his neck to check on the black horse who was now securely detained by Casey's rope. Then he looked the pony in the eye. "Good boy," he whispered and patted him on the forehead.

Lisa took a breath and mouthed the words, "Thank you."

I turned back to Casey. "What do we do now?"

"Well, we can't leave him out here. I can't take a chance at having that happen again. And I have no idea where he came from." The black horse whipped its head back and forth and pawed at the ground. "Lucy, can you lead these guys back? I'll follow and hopefully we can get this horse back down to the ranch. Then we'll figure it out from there."

"Yes...yes, I can do that." I gathered my thoughts and my reins. "Simon, can you and Sharkie help me lead this trail? I really need your help."

Simon stared at me and then slowly nodded his head. He wiped his runny nose on his sleeve, took hold of Sharkie's reins and put a boot in the stirrup.

FOUR

BACK AT THE barn, I rushed to tie the horses to the fence. I yanked their saddles off and threw the tack in a pile on the grass. "Come on, girl," I said, clucking at Sunny and pulling her towards the pasture. Sunny didn't seem to be as rattled as I was, but she trotted anyhow.

"What's the rush, Lucy?" Marilynn asked, walking out of the barn.

I didn't turn around. I closed the gate behind Sunny and hurried back to the other horses. "Hello!" Marilynn yelled, waving her hands in the air. "Did you hear what I just said?"

"Casey roped a horse...a crazy black horse." I started untying Freckle's lead from the fence.

"What are you talking about? We don't even have a black horse on the ranch." Marilynn's face scrunched up, ready to scream profanities at me, when a high pitched whinny shrieked from behind the barn. We both stopped in our tracks and whipped around.

"That...*that* is what I am talking about."

The black horse was dripping sweat, but still fighting. Head raised, he whinnied again, prancing and pulling his weight against the rope. Poor Rocky was getting jerked and pulled on, but he just kept walking.

"What are we supposed to do with that?" Marilynn asked, staring at the mess of a horse as it approached the barn.

"Open one of the barn paddocks," Casey directed, still wrestling with the rope. The horse seemed to be fighting with the same grueling intensity. Casey had to be exhausted by now.

"You're going to put that thing in the barn?" Marilynn questioned him. "Are you crazy?"

"I don't know what else to do with him. He's just going to cause problems if we let him go."

Marilynn shook her head. "Fine. Put him in the last paddock. He shouldn't bother any of the other horses over there, but I swear I'm going to freak if he kicks through the barn walls."

I sprinted towards the barn, leaving Freckles tied, and swung the paddock gate open. There were ten individual paddocks, each connected by a dutch door to a barn stall, but they were reserved for the guests' horses. On the opposite end of the barn, Star barreled out of her stall. Assessing the situation, she pranced around her paddock, tail held high, adding unneeded chaos.

Casey tried coaxing the black horse into the paddock, but he balked at the sight of the open gate. Every muscle in his body stiffened and his hooves dug into the gravel, refusing to move forward. From a safe distance behind, Marilynn and I waved our hands in the air. *Just take a few steps forward. Get in there. Get in there.*

And then he did, by grand scale. The black horse leapt straight to the sky, soaring over an invisible jump, and landed square in the middle of the paddock, frozen.

In the few seconds he was still, distracted by his surroundings, Casey grabbed the loop of his rope. At his touch, the horse reversed at light speed, ramming his hind end into the fence, but Casey held tight and the rope popped off the horse's head. Turning Rocky, Casey hustled him out the gate and I slammed it shut.

And there the black horse stood. His feet planted firm on the ground, afraid to move. His coat dripped in sweat and a stark white rim lined his eyes. All three of us gawked at his sudden silence. The rattling metal gate was now the only sound.

"Well, we got him in there. Now what do you suggest we do?" Marilynn crossed her arms, looking back and forth between Casey and me. "Mr. Owens is not going to want a crazy, wild horse running around in his barn."

"I think he would like it even less if that crazy horse chased down his guests *again*," Casey shot back, tired of her lip.

"He chased you down?" Marilynn glared at the black horse, tapping the toe of her boot. "Well, you guys figure it out. And, please figure it out quickly... before Mr. Owens gets involved."

At that, Marilynn marched back to the barn without another word.

Casey sighed, dismounting from Rocky. "Well, she's not very happy with me," he said, wiping his forehead with a handkerchief.

"We did the right thing. We couldn't just leave him up there. Who knows what would happen the next time we rode through." I paused, looking at the black horse. "And he's lost. Somebody has got to be looking for him. Even if he is crazy."

"Yeah, you're probably right," Casey agreed, stuffing his handkerchief back in his pocket. "By the way, you did a great job out there."

The random compliment broke my thoughts and I turned to face him. "You roped a wild horse and pulled it down a mountain. What did I do?"

"You pulled that little boy out of the way before I could even get my rope in the air. It could have been a total disaster if you hadn't been there with me." His blue eyes actually looked sincere.

"Thanks," I said, squirming under the unneeded compliments.

The black horse whinnied again, but this time he sounded shaky and unsure. "He's going to need a bucket of water and some hay after he cools down."

"I'll get it," I offered. "Go take care of Rocky. He looks like he needs a hose down."

"Thanks, kid." Casey smiled and held my gaze just long enough to make me uncomfortable.

Four-thirty-six Sunday morning and I was staring at the blinking numbers on my alarm clock. Rolling over, I slid the quilt over my head, trying to force my body to sleep. Just one more hour. Squeezing my eyes shut for a few more minutes, I decided it was useless. There were too many images racing through my head. I pictured that black horse, drenched in sweat, standing alone in his paddock, scared out of his mind...and I hoped he was okay. Throwing my covers back, I sat straight-up in bed. I needed to check on him.

Outside, a pink haze outlined the mountain and rain pattered on the grass. The quiet was eerie yet comforting as I headed along the path. The barn door squeaked as I rolled it open and Star nickered a soft welcome. She looked cozy in her pink plaid sheet, but I didn't let her sweet face fool me this time. I threw a few flakes of hay over her stall door before she could flashed her teeth at me.

I tiptoed down the dim aisle, not wanting to scare the black horse, but I didn't hear a single noise as I approached the last stall. The horse hadn't kicked the wall, pawed at the floor, or even given his shrill whinny. Peering over the door, I scanned his stall. It was empty. The bucket of water and his hay were untouched. My gut sank. Marilynn is going to freak if he broke through the fence and ran off.

I quickly opened the door to assess the damage, but, at my entrance, something banged hard against the paddock fence. I focused my eyes past the stall and into the attached paddock...and there the black horse stood, pressed against the fence and soaking wet in the drizzling rain.

I crept further into the stall. There was not one hoof print in the shavings. He had been out there all night. Why wouldn't he come out of the rain and into the barn?

Putting both flakes of hay under my arm, I picked up the water bucket and walked towards the paddock. I didn't take my eyes off the black horse as I remembered what he was like yesterday. One quick movement from him and I would be jumping for the door.

But, he didn't move. He watched me as I set the bucket and the hay just outside the stall and then we stared at each other.

His drenched coat emphasized his ribby sides. "You should really eat something," I whispered and backed away, locking the stall door behind me. I couldn't believe he stood out in the cold rain all night when he could've slept in a warm, dry stall with a belly full of hay.

Out of his sight in the barn aisle, I munched on my strawberry pop tart and looked around for something to do while I waited for Marilynn. *The tack could use a good cleaning, I guess.* Grabbing a bridle, rag, and leather cleaner from the tack room, I took a seat on the long wooden bench. I was about to turn on the radio when I heard the slightest bit of rustling from the end of the barn.

Setting the bridle down, I tiptoed along the stall fronts and peeked over the black horse's stall door. The sun was coming up and I could now easily see into the paddock. The black horse was just outside the stall with his head to the ground, carefully wrapping his lips around a few strands of hay. He stretched his neck out, keeping his body a safe distance from the foreign building. But, when he finished chewing, he stepped one foot closer and ripped a big mouthful, shaking his head and spreading the flake at his feet.

I held my breath, making sure not to giggle at his overzealous bite. I didn't want to alert him of my hiding spot and I watched in silence as the black horse filled his hungry belly. Standing there, chewing on his hay, he didn't look scary or mean. He just looked frightened...unsure.

The black horse ate a portion of the hay and then dipped his nose in the water bucket and gulped. Ripples of skin ran up the bottom of his neck as he drank. When there was nothing left, he raised his head and licked his wet lips, water dripping from his whiskered muzzle. He finally seemed content.

Just then, the barn door to my left swung open and chaos took over. In one swift movement, the horse spun on his hind legs, sent his bucket flying, and lunged himself to the farthest point of the paddock. In the commotion, I tried to step backwards, but, instead, tripped over my own feet and landed on my butt facing Marilynn.

Marilynn stepped through the door and pulled back the hood of her yellow raincoat.

"What are you doing?" Marilynn looked at me with one eyebrow cocked and then turned to peer into the stall. "And what is that crazy horse doing?"

I stood up and brushed the dirt from my jeans, feeling a bit silly. "He was eating. I moved his hay out in the paddock because he won't come into the stall. I think he's scared of the barn."

Marilynn's eyebrow rose further. Then she turned to survey the stall and what she could see of the paddock. "He didn't destroy anything overnight?"

"Doesn't look like it." I shrugged my shoulders.

"Well, that's a plus. Maybe it's better if he stays out of the barn."

I looked at the black horse, pushed up against the end of the puddled paddock. The white around his eyes had returned and he was on full alert again, staring at us. I felt like I needed to stick up for him, but I didn't know what to say.

I carried on with morning chores without a mention of the black horse, but managed a glance in his stall each time I passed by. Throughout the morning, his mound of hay slowly disappeared and I didn't witness any more commotion. Hopefully, that meant he was settling in.

Sunday was a quiet day on the ranch. Marilynn and I finished chores and there weren't any trail rides scheduled for the afternoon. Instead, I spent the extra time pampering the ranch horses. A bucket of brushes in hand, I moved from one horse to the next, making my way through the pasture. Each horse got their share of rubbing as I combed their manes and curried their bodies while they napped in the afternoon sun.

After the evening feeding, I walked the trail back to my bunk. The rain and fog had burned off by noon and the sun was glowing in the open sky. It was only six o'clock and I had no idea what I was going to do for the rest of the evening. Contemplating the task of organizing my bunk, I remembered Marilynn mentioned a bonfire at the main lodge. She said everyone was welcome. *It wouldn't hurt to check it out.*

A quick wardrobe change and a baseball hat later, my bunk's screen door slapped shut behind me. There was no way I could sit inside and ignore the summer weather.

Past the outdoor arena, I made my way up the hill towards the main lodge. The long log cabin sat squarely against the mountain backdrop. A covered porch wrapped the front of the cabin and a handful of guests swayed and chatted on wooden rocking chairs. A trail of smoke rose from the massive stone fireplace, protruding from the middle of the roof, and country music hummed through the air. I took a deep breath and could taste the campfire.

The music started to blare as I walked around the back corner of the lodge, setting my eyes on an orange blaze. A massive bonfire roared in the cozy circle of land between the back of the lodge and the multiple guest cabins. And, a dancing mass of people bounced to the music of three guitars, a violin, and a sassy female singer.

The band was perched on the lodge's back deck and their catchy tunes forced my head to bob in rhythm. The upbeat country music reminded me of home and I started my way through the dancing crowd, scanning the back deck for a place to sit. But, instead of a seat, I got a sharp elbow to the ribs from a little spinning flash of blonde curls.

"Watch where you are going," Taylor snapped, her face just inches from mine, but she barely made eye contact before spinning back into the arms of a waiting cowboy.

Slightly stunned by her lack of manners, I stood there watching as the dancing couple rocked back into seamless rhythm. His hand found the small of her back and Taylor threw her slender arm around his broad shoulders. Reaching up, she snatched the black cowboy hat from his head and placed it on her own. Hatless, her dancing partner brushed his sandy brown hair out of his eyes as Taylor swayed her hips to her own beat.

The sandy haired cowboy was Casey.

I couldn't get out of there fast enough. I turned to retreat, but there were dancing couples in every direction.

In the midst of my shuffling, Casey caught my eye. "Lucy?" he asked, peering through the mob.

Trapped, I stood in the crowd feeling like a stalker. *I should have stayed in my bunk.*

I waved my hand and forced a smile, still looking for somewhere to retreat, but Casey made his way towards me. Taylor was close behind.

"Hey, glad you decided to come to the bonfire. Pretty fun, huh?" Casey's smile was welcoming, but it didn't make me feel any more comfortable.

"Pretty fun," I responded, avoiding Taylor's glare as she stood at Casey's side. Even without eye contact, I felt her looking me up and down, accusing me of something hideous.

"How's the black horse doing?" Casey asked, oblivious to Taylor's stares.

"Pretty freaked out," I said. "But he's eating and drinking now. And, he hasn't broken anything in the barn so far."

"That's good," Casey nodded. "Wanted to let you

know I stopped by the sheriff's office earlier today. Asked if anyone reported a lost horse, but no one has. I left a description of the black horse and told the sheriff he was at the ranch if anyone came looking for him."

My mind raced back to images of the frightened horse. "I'm not really sure how someone loses their horse, but hopefully they can find him now."

Casey shrugged. "I'm not sure either, but he's got a place to stay while we figure it out."

"Sarah?" Taylor burst out the question as though she hadn't listened to a word of our conversation.

Casey and I both stopped and looked at her.

"Excuse me?" I asked when she didn't say anything else.

"Sarah. You're the new girl working at the barn." She said, like she was proud to remember who I was.

"Lucy," I responded.

"Lucy, Sarah. Close enough," Taylor said, rolling her eyes.

As the band started a new song, Taylor fully lost interest in our conversation.

"Let's dance!" she squeaked and tugged at Casey's arm.

Casey opened his mouth, but no words came out before Taylor pulled him back into the crowd. I was left standing by myself, again. *Sarah...that is not even remotely close to my name.*

I maneuvered a path to the deck and half-listened

to another song. I watched everyone dance and laugh around the bonfire. And, the more I watched, the more I felt like I didn't belong. Feeling homesick for the first time, I snuck out and headed back in the direction of my bunk.

With the country music fading in the background, the ranch felt cold and quiet. The sun had set and there wasn't another soul within ear shot. My empty bunk didn't sound too appealing either.

Maybe I should check on the black horse? Being in the barn would be much better than sitting in my bunk by myself.

I shuffled down the barn aisle to the black horse's stall and peeked inside, trying not to scare him again. In the paddock, he nibbled on the last strands of his hay, but, when he noticed my presence, he whipped his head up and backed a few quick steps.

"It's okay, boy. I just came to check on you." I said, resting my arms on his stall door. I let him assess me in silence and, after a few minutes, crept inside the stall to sit down in the unused cedar bedding.

"You know, this bedding is pretty comfortable. You should give it a try," I said, resting my head against the stall boards and wrapping by arms around my knees.

The black horse didn't move. He stared at me, his ears pricked forward and head cocked. "I know how you feel," I whispered, watching him in the paddock. "It's kind of scary being away from home, but it will be okay. You don't have to be scared." I took a deep breath, half-reassuring myself of the same thing. "We'll find your owner. Don't you worry."

The black horse blinked his eyes and stepped closer to his hay. He never took his eyes off me, but seemed to accept that I wasn't a threat...at the moment.

In the quiet, I pictured Taylor's blank face as I reminded her of my name. She really didn't care what my name was. I'm not sure why that irritated me, but it did.

The black horse chewed his hay.

"Black horse...you deserve a name. You deserve to be called something other than black horse." I twiddled my thumbs, trying to think of a fitting name. "You deserve a name no one will forget."

He needed something strong. Something to give him confidence. *Thunder? No, too intimidating. Ebony? No, that's not quite right.*

"You just need a chance to prove yourself."

The black horse cocked his head again at my whispered statement.

"Chance? Do you like that?"

The black horse picked his head up from his hay, nodding up and down. He was probably just shoeing a fly from his nose, but I took it as a sign that he liked the name. That he would choose that name for himself. And I thought it fit.

"Chance it is," I smiled. "Thanks for keeping me

company, Chance."

FIVE

MONDAY FLEW BY. I finished feeding the horses and cleaning stalls just in time to saddle up with Marilynn for the scheduled afternoon trail ride. Again, I tailed the end of the ride on Sunny, but today's adventure was less eventful than yesterday's...there was no charging wild horse and no one cried.

As the sun set, I helped Marilynn load the saddles back in the tack room.

"I can't believe how late it is already," Marilynn said as she heaved the last saddle on the wooden rack. "I'm starving."

"Me too," I said as my stomach growled. I hadn't noticed any hunger pains until Marilynn mentioned food.

Scanning the tack room, Marilynn nodded. "Okay. We're done for the day. Let's go ransack the kitchen."

I followed her lead.

With a belly full of homemade chili and a stack of chocolate chip cookies in my hand, I walked through my bunk door and slumped down on my bed. My body felt like jelly but, even as tired as I was, the silence in my bunk was overwhelming. With the excitement of the day slipping away, the homesick pangs returned.

Trying to ignore them, I grabbed *SummerDust*, the book sitting on my night stand, and picked up where I left off last night. It was the third book in my favorite series and I was sentences away from the start of the Kentucky Derby. I read on as Summer, the longshot filly with the big heart, entered the starting gate, but placed the open book on my chest when I realized even the suspense of the race couldn't keep my attention.

The silence surrounding me was deafening. It gave me too much room to think. I closed my eyes, hoping for a food-coma to kick in. *You're fine. Just tough it out. You'll get used to being here. You'll make friends. Just think about the time you get to spend in the barn, with the horses, in the saddle. Keep thinking about that.*

So I did. And, as I laid there thinking about the horses, I realized there was someone else at the ranch fighting my same battle...Chance. He was away from home and he didn't know anyone either. *Maybe we could wallow in our newness together?*

The next evening, when Marilynn said good night, I grabbed my dinner to-go and made my way to the barn.

"Hey there," I whispered, sliding open Chance's stall door. My entrance wasn't loud enough to startle a mouse, but Chance stumbled backwards and then stared at me from the paddock, neck arched and eyes wide. I stepped inside the stall, trying to ignore his not-so-welcoming demeanor.

"You mind if I have dinner with you?" I asked, half-looking for an approval. When Chance didn't move, I found a comfy spot in his clean bedding and sat down cross-legged to unwrap my tuna salad sandwich. Most horses would be curious as to why I decided to sit on their stall floor. They would mosey close and sniff me all over. Probably try to nibble on my dinner or nuzzle my hair. But, Chance wasn't like most horses. He stood in his paddock like a coal black statue. He didn't even blink.

I took a bite out of my sandwich anyhow.

I chewed and let my eyes slide shut. The quiet here was different. It wasn't foreign like my bunk. The barn was filled with sounds of rustling hay and soft snorts. The scent of sweet grass and cedar bedding filled my lungs. And, being near Chance felt familiar, even if he wasn't as warm & cozy as my Stella at home. Even if he didn't want to come near me.

Lost in the comfort of the barn, my eyes jerked

open when a crunching noise snuck up on me. I yanked my legs out from underneath myself, scrambling to jump for safety. Images of flailing black hooves flashed through my mind. But, turning my head towards the paddock, I froze with my feet out in front of me, realizing Chance had only taken a few steps closer. His neck lowered, he watched my every move, eyes wide with a mouth full of hay.

"Geez," I exhaled and rested my arms against my knees. "You scared the crap out of me." Touching my hand to my thumping chest, I was amazed I avoided a heart attack. "For a second there, I thought I was going to see the bottom of your feet."

Chance continued staring at me, hay pieces sticking out of both sides of his mouth. Certain I wasn't going to get up, he started chewing.

I shook my head and chuckled. "You almost made me choke on my tuna salad sandwich."

The next few evenings I spent in Chance's stall, eating my dinner and telling him stories. I told him anything that came to mind and he listened, from a distance, as he chewed his hay. I told him about Stella, my mare at home, and the home cooked dinners my grandma makes every Sunday. I told him about Taylor and her mare's sour attitude. And I told him how Casey ended up with Rocky. Chance kept his eyes on me through every story, hanging on each word. He still wouldn't come within ten feet of me, but I did notice a few hoof prints in his stall bedding. Maybe our evening talks were starting to make him feel comfortable too.

Back at work, I unclasped Star's halter and shut the gate to one of the smaller pastures. She pranced away from me, shaking her head and hopping around in the afternoon sun. Her flaxen mane rolled in the breeze as her hooves sprung from the ground. I smiled as she put her nose to the grass and began nibbling.

Throwing the halter over my shoulder, I turned back towards the barn, but stopped in my tracks as I witnessed the chaos. In a blur of black, Chance ran back and forth at end of his paddock, frantic and screaming. A man in a cowboy hat and jean jacket walked towards him with a halter and lead dangling from his hand. Chance reared up and I held my breath until his feet reluctantly hit the ground. He was either going to jump over the fence or go through it. I took off in a dead sprint for the barn.

Marilynn stood at the front of Chance's stall and watched me as I raced down the aisle.

"What's going on?" I yelled, hoping that man hadn't gotten any closer to Chance. Marilynn opened her mouth to respond, but I didn't wait for her words. I pushed open the stall door and scrambled inside.

The man was still walking towards Chance, now with his hands held high in the air, giving Chance nowhere to go. Chance crashed his shoulder against the metal gate, making it ring, and when the man didn't retreat, he reared towards the cowboy, feet flailing and ears pinned flat. I was too late. Somebody was going to get hurt.

"You can't do that!" I screamed from the stall just as the man shielded his face with his arms and ran backwards.

Unharmed, he turned and stomped past me into the barn aisle. "Apparently not," he said, tossing the halter and lead on the ground and staring back at Chance. "I was just trying to catch him," the man stated, wiping his wrinkled brow with a handkerchief. "What is *wrong* with that horse?"

Marilynn shot me a glare as I stepped into the aisle and shut the stall door. Chance ran back and forth at the end of the paddock as though the man was still in there with him. A cloud of dust circled his legs and clung to his sweaty body. My heart pounded in my ears.

The startled man was in his sixties, tall and trim. Silver sideburns poked out from underneath his black cowboy hat. His hands were rough, but clean as though he had worked hard in his life, but not in some time. "We can't have something like that here at the ranch." He directed his statement at Marilynn. "He's a law suit waiting to happen."

"I know, Mr. Owens," Marilynn responded. "He's only been here a few days. Casey has been checking with the sheriff's office to see if anyone has reported a lost horse, but no one has. I'm not sure what to do with him."

"Let's try to get him loaded in the stock trailer and I'll haul him over to the livestock auction in Three Rivers."

An auction? I looked back at Chance, pacing and pawing at the fence, practically frothing at the mouth. No one would buy him. No one would take the time to see the good in him. He'd end up getting shipped off to slaughter.

"Please...please let him stay," I blurted out as my gut flipped.

Mr. Owens stared at me for a few hard seconds. "And you are?"

"This is Lucy Rose," Marilynn jumped in and flashed me a look like I had better shut my mouth. "She was hired to help me with the horses for the summer. Lucy, *this* is Mr. Owen's. This is his ranch."

I swallowed what little spit was left in my mouth, wishing I had made a better first impression.

Mr. Owens brushed the dust from his weathered jean jacket. "Every horse here earns their keep and I can't have one just standing around eating hay and taking up space. Not to mention, he could hurt someone."

"He's just scared." I said, wondering if Mr. Owens and Marilynn could hear my voice waver. "He needs some work."

"That's an understatement," Mr. Owens replied, wide-eyed and searching my face for a better answer.

"I'll work with him," I offered. "I'll do it. He just

needs time. I'm sure he could make a great ranch horse." Both of their mouths dropped open.

I wasn't sure my statement even made sense. I didn't know if Chance could be broke...or even touched for that matter, but I did know Chance didn't deserve to be shipped off to an auction. Mr. Owens owned the ranch, the horses, the cattle. He must have a soft spot for the animals or he wouldn't have them. My eyes shifted between Marilynn and Mr. Owens, waiting for a response.

Mr. Owens sighed, shaking his head. "Fine. The auction isn't for two weeks. If I took him to the stockyards now, I'd have to pay to keep him stalled until the auction." He looked me straight in the eye. "You have two weeks to work with him. If you can't get him broke in that time we will have no choice but to take him to auction."

"I understand. Thank you, Mr. Owens," I said, as he turned his back to me and walked out of the barn.

Marilynn stood in the same spot with her hands pressed firmly on her hips. She closed her mouth, only to start snapping her gum. "You might be crazier than that horse. What exactly do you think you are going to do with him?"

We turned to stare at Chance who had worked himself into a dripping, frothy sweat.

"I don't really know what I am going to do with him," I whispered as he continued pacing in his paddock.

Marilynn and Casey rode off with a group of guests on an afternoon trail ride and I was in charge of cleaning up the barn. I picked the stalls, swept the aisle, and organized the tack room. Satisfied with my work, I made my way to Chance's stall, hoping he had calmed down after this morning's episode with Mr. Owens.

Chance's head hung low and heavy as he stood in his paddock. The once-frothy sweat had dried and chalk white lines were left in its place. That poor boy needed to be brushed. He needed a good bath. He needed some love. But, how could I do any of that if I couldn't even get close to him?

Maybe I couldn't tame him, but I knew I had to buy Chance time until I could find out where he came from. Somehow, he was far away from home, lost and scared.

I tossed a few flakes of hay into his paddock and sat cross-legged in his stall. Chance stared at me, his eyes glazed over with exhaustion. "I'm not going to chase you, Chance. Don't worry. Eat your hay."

Chance watched me for a few silent minutes, and when I didn't move, he moved to the hay. He nibbled, but kept his dark eyes on me. His ears flicked towards each noise in the background, but pointed in my directions as my stomach gurgled.

"Did you hear that?" I asked him, realizing I forgot to eat lunch. "I guess it was pretty loud."

Good thing I carried a reserve. Reaching in my pocket, I pulled out a peanut butter granola bar and ripped open the crinkly silver wrapper. Enjoying my first chewy bite, I noticed Chance extending his neck, just a few inches. His nostrils flared with small puffs of air as he tried to identify the new smell.

"Does that smell good?" I mumbled as I tore off a chunk and offered it in my flat hand. "It's peanut butter."

I reached my hand out as far as possible without leaving my seat on the stall floor. Chance balked at my gesture.

"I'm not going to hurt you, Chance," I whispered, holding my hand still. *I wonder how long I can keep this position.*

And, as I contemplated, Chance began to inch closer. His hooves were planted firmly on the ground, but he reached his nose out, farther and farther, until he was inches from my hand. I held my breath as he sniffed and nuzzled the unknown item with his whiskered top lip...and then he snatched it from my hand. His lower jaw moved in tiny circles, grinding the granola bar. His head bobbed up and down as he finished the treat and then he stood there, staring at me, ignoring the pile of hay at his feet.

I ripped off another piece of the granola bar, but froze when I heard voices outside the barn. Chance's ears pricked forward and he stepped back. *Dang. They must be back from the trail ride already.*

Sighing, I stood up and brushed the bedding from my backside. *I wish I had just a little more time alone with Chance.*

"Hey, Lucy," Casey said, breaking my thought as he walked down the barn aisle, bridles hanging from his shoulder. "How's the black horse doing?"

I glanced at the gelding that was just inches from my fingers. "Better. He's better."

"Good to hear," Casey said, pulling open the stall door to get a better look.

"Have you heard anything from the sheriff's office?"

Casey shook his head. "Still nothing. I just can't believe no one around here is looking for a lost horse. If Rocky went missing, I would be calling every neighbor and police station within a hundred miles. I don't get it." Casey shrugged his shoulders and his eyes drifted towards the paddock.

"I don't get it either," I agreed, watching Chance chew a few yellow strands of hay.

Casey leaned his shoulder against the stall door, looping his thumbs in his jeans pockets. "So, Marilynn told me about your introduction to Mr. Owens this morning."

I stopped breathing. *Great. Casey thinks I'm crazy too.*

"That was pretty bold," Casey noted.

I met his eyes. Bold? Was that a nice way of calling me stupid? I searched for a way to explain myself, to explain Chance, to tell Casey that I really didn't know what I was doing...but I stopped as a warm smile graced Casey's face.

"I'm excited to see a change in that black horse. Glad you're up for the challenge."

I mulled over Casey's use of the word challenge, but was thankful someone was taking my side. "Thanks," I whispered.

"And let me know if you need any help," Casey offered as he turned towards the tack room, pulling the dusty brim of his baseball hat over his eyes.

"Hey, Casey?" I called after him and poked my head out the stall door. "I don't want to call him the black horse anymore. He deserves a name...and I thought we could call him Chance."

Casey nodded. "I think that sounds perfect."

SIX

CHANCE'S BLACK NOSE wrinkled as his wet tongue rolled across the palm of my hand. A smile grew on my face, but I kept from giggling. My secret weapon, the peanut butter granola bar, had cast a surprising spell on Chance.

This was the third evening attempting this trick-- breaking a bar into several small pieces and waiting patiently as each treat lured Chance closer and closer. Kneeling on the stall floor, Chance's breath warmed my open palm. He was as close as he had ever been and I couldn't help but to touch him. I brushed his muzzle with my fingertips and Chance jerked his head sideways, shooting an accusatory glare my way.

I lowered my hand. "You've got to trust me, Chance. You have to trust me so I can help you." Sighing, I repeated the words again in a soft rhythm as

I raised my opposite arm, offering another piece of granola bar, this time with a halter and lead dangling from my forearm.

Chance arched his neck at the foreign object, but was fully aware of the treat before him. "Trust me, Buddy. Trust me," I whispered and his ears flicked forward again. Unable to resist the bar, Chance lowered his muzzle to my hand and, as he relished in the treat, I slipped my hand past his nose to hold it against his cheek.

Chance stopped chewing and we stared at each other. Touching and eye-to-eye, I became terribly aware how close this thousand pound animal was to me. My head told me to back off, but my heart wouldn't let me. I didn't pull away...and neither did Chance. Frozen in silence. Each of us waited for the other to make a move.

And then Chance did. He started chewing again. He didn't run away. He didn't throw his head. He just watched me and chewed and my hand moved with the circular motion of his jaw.

I grabbed another treat from my pocket and Chance lapped it up without hesitation. Happy with our progress, I began humming along with the country music playing on the barn radio and I slowly stood, rolling my hand up to his neck.

I pushed back his tangled mane and stroked his smooth, black coat. I'm not sure if it was the humming or the rubbing, but Chance licked his lips, a sign of relaxation. I blew a tense breath from my lungs.

I hummed every song from the radio's top-ten countdown and rubbed on Chance until my shoulders ached and the sun set behind Mount Hood. With his head lowered and eyes droopy, Chance didn't seem to notice as I slipped the halter over his nose and quietly clasped it behind his ears.

"Now, let's take that ratty leather collar off of you." I said wiggling the rusty buckle and pushing until the leather broke free of the metal. The attached plastic tag, marked with a number thirteen, broke in half as the collar hit the ground. Good riddance.

I studied Chance, sporting the new nylon halter. "You look good in royal blue," I smiled.

Chance cocked his head towards me, blinking those big brown eyes. "Okay, I'll hum you one more song and then I have got to get some sleep."

That night I pulled my covers up to my chin and fell right to sleep. And, I dreamed of being on Chance's back, galloping through the open mountain field where the cattle grazed. The cool air rushed into my lungs and whipped through my hair. Chance's black neck stretched out in front of me and his body moved under mine splitting the tall grass. Each powerful stride felt like an achievement. Nothing could have felt better.

Then my alarm clock screamed and ripped me from my fantasy. I slammed the snooze button and pulled a pillow over my head, aching to go back to sleep. I needed to fall back into my dream...even for five more minutes. Why did 5:30 have to come so fast?

I laid there in protest, refusing to get up, thinking about Chance. Coming out of my sleepy haze, I remembered our evening together and couldn't believe I got a halter on him. It was a far cry from galloping through the fields, but at least we were moving in the right direction.

And, this afternoon I have a few open hours while Marilynn takes out a trail ride. In fact, she told me to get working on *that black horse* while she is gone. Apparently, Mr. Owens was asking for updates and Marilynn couldn't bring herself to tell him I didn't even have him out of the paddock yet.

But I did get a halter on him yesterday and I wanted to try a saddle today.

The afternoon sun beat hard on my shoulders as we made our trek from Chance's paddock to the arena. Chance cautiously followed my lead and second-guessed every distraction along the way. He jumped sideways when the wind rustled the bushes, baulked at a funny looking rock, and just about lost it when a squirrel crossed our path. I kept coaxing him, hoping he wouldn't bolt back towards the barn, taking me with him.

By the time we walked through the arena gate, my arms were sore from getting yanked around and my grand idea of galloping through the mountain seemed decades away. Needless to say, I was *not excited* to find Taylor in our destination. I didn't need an audience for this. Especially an audience made up of Taylor Johnson.

Taylor loped past us without even a glance in our direction. Star was tacked up in an English saddle with a zebra print saddle pad and matching leg wraps. Taylor donned tan breeches and a black velvet helmet. She steered Star towards a two foot jump and they breezed over it like it was nothing.

Rounding the arena, Taylor took notice of Chance and trotted over, posting in the saddle.

"Are you going to stand there?" she asked, stopping Star in front of us.

"Excuse me?" I responded. Did this girl know how to say hello?

"Are you going to stand right *there*?" Taylor repeated, slower. "You're kind of in the way of my jump."

I tried to process her rude attitude, but decided it would be best not to start a fight with one of the ranch's guests. "I'll stay out of your way," I stated, wondering if she ever learned how to share. "I didn't know you jumped Star."

Taylor fiddled with the chin strap on her helmet. "We just started training before we headed here for the summer. Kind of bored with the rodeo queen thing at the moment," she shrugged.

Taylor didn't look like she was just learning how to jump. She looked like she could walk into a show ring and win the class.

"Is that the wild horse that Casey roped?" Taylor asked as she eyed up Chance. "Looks a little rough around the edges."

"His name is Chance," I informed her.

"Chance...like half-a-chance?" Her overly white teeth gleamed in the sun as she laughed at her own joke, shaking her head.

My mouth gapped open. Who did this little brat think she was? I turned on my heels and clucked to Chance before my mouth spewed out what I really wanted to say.

"Oh, come on. It was just a joke," Taylor whined as I walked past.

I just kept walking. How could Casey possibly be interested in that girl? Her pretty face masked a nasty attitude. The more I got to know her, the more I disliked her. She was not nice. In fact, she was downright mean. But, maybe Casey was too entranced by her blonde hair and perfect body to care?

I watched Taylor jump Star again, in flawless form, as I lead Chance towards saddle and brushes I dropped off earlier. Stopping him at the fence, I grabbed a rubber curry and started rubbing circles on his neck. He stiffened, for a second, and then gave in to the massaging action of the curry.

Chance sniffed the saddle hanging on the fence,

blowing short breathes over the leather.

"Are you going to let me put that on you today?" I asked, pushing Taylor's comments out of my head.

Now that I was gaining his trust, this could be easy. In fact, he could be trained under-saddle for all I know. But, it was also possible he had never seen a saddle. Today might turn into a rodeo bronc show. My heart beat picked up at the thought.

I grabbed the saddle pad and rubbed it all over Chance's body, getting him use to the feel of the coarse wool. He didn't flinch. I kept rubbing until I noticed Taylor riding out of the arena. She was on her cell phone and giggling about something. At least we wouldn't have an audience.

"Okay, let's give this a shot."

I positioned the pad on Chance's back and pulled the saddle off the fence. I held my breath as I gently placed the heavy leather saddle on his back. I let go, allowing the saddle's full weight to rest on Chance and, to my surprise, he didn't move. He didn't do anything except watch me with his left eye.

I looked for any sign of body language as I tightened the girth, waiting for Chance to explode. Still nothing. I took a step back and looked him over. He was quiet. Almost frozen. Not the reaction I was expecting.

Maybe I was making a bigger deal out of this than I needed to be.

"Good boy, Chance," I whispered, taking a breath

and placing one foot in the stirrup. I paused as I pressed my body weight on the saddle. If he exploded, I could still jump back. But, he had no reaction. It was almost spooky, how quiet he was.

I grabbed hold of the saddle horn and swung my body into the seat, quickly putting my other foot in the stirrup. I had the lead in one hand and both hands wrapped around the saddle horn, expecting the worst.

Chance was like a solid statue. Not moving. He didn't even seem curious as to why I was on top of him.

I lightly squeezed my legs together and clucked my tongue.

"Let's try walking, boy." I clucked again, trying to give him some motivation.

Nothing. It was like sitting on a rock.

I went to squeeze him again, but I must have hit a different button...because I got the reaction I was initially expecting. Plus a little more.

Chance didn't explode. He shattered.

He reverted back to the first day I met him. Putting his head to the ground, Chance launched himself forward so hard that my chest slammed against the saddle horn as his feet returned to the ground. I didn't have time to react as his throat made a primitive guttural noise and all four hooves cut through the air, kicking out with such force that I simply couldn't hang on.

My body unwillingly flipped through the air and

all I saw was the arena dirt. I landed hard, face down, the wind pushed from my lungs.

Then, moving only on instinct, I rolled as fast as my body would let me, avoiding flailing hooves.

At a safe distance from the explosion, I pushed myself to my hands and knees and spit the earthy dirt from my mouth.

"Oh my God! Are you okay?" Taylor shrieked as she trotted Star over and closed her cell phone.

I didn't respond right away, partially because I had no air left in my lungs. "I'm okay," I forced out, but I wasn't sure if I was. Adrenaline pumped through my veins, but it didn't numb the throbbing pain in my shoulder or the sharp imprint the saddle horn left in my chest.

"What is wrong with that horse?" Taylor asked, scrunching her face up in disgust instead of concern.

I crawled to a kneeling position and tried to brush the dirt from the front of my tank top, but it was useless. I must have skidded across the ground when I hit. Dirt ground against my skin, under my clothes, as I moved.

I patted my body, checking for signs of broken bones or blood. And, when I was sure I was in one piece, Chance's rodeo show came to a halt. He stood facing us from a distance, his sides heaving and white blaring in his eyes.

"It's not his fault," I sighed, shaking my head. *Stupid, stupid, stupid.* "I pushed him too fast."

"Umm, he just put your face in the ground," Taylor said, accenting the word *face*. I didn't need a reminder. "I'd be pissed if I were you."

I couldn't concern myself with Taylor right now. Limping myself into a standing position, I wiped my grimy face and moved towards Chance. I crept across the arena and Chance leaned his body weight backwards, ready to run again. When I snatched up the end of the lead rope, dangling on the ground, Chance propelled backwards.

"Easy, Easy, boy," I pleaded and followed, holding tight to the end of the lead rope. "It's okay, Chance. It's okay. I promise." And, thankfully, Chance slowed his feet as he realized I wasn't mad...at him.

"Have fun with that mess," Taylor said, turning to walk Star out of the arena.

How stupid of me. I should have taken more time to get him used to the saddle. He was scared frozen. I pushed him too hard. It was my fault.

I loosened the girth and slid the saddle from Chance's back, dropping it to the ground and fighting back every feeling of defeat.

Back in the barn, I closed Chance's stall door and leaned against it, processing what just happened. I'd never been on a horse that bucked like that. I could have gotten hurt. I could have gotten Chance hurt. My head spun with the frightening possibilities that hadn't happened.

"What the heck happened to you?" Marilynn asked, walking out of the tack room and stopping abruptly, her eyes as big as saucers. I was sure I looked like a complete mess, dirt smeared across my face and ground into my clothes. I tilted my head to the ceiling, fighting the tears building in my eyes.

"I hit the dirt," I squeaked out, wiping the tears from my cheeks. The back of my hand slid across the grit on my face.

"Well, that's obvious," Marilynn stated, approaching the stall. Then she pointed an accusing finger at Chance. "Did he do that to you?"

I shook my head, letting out a long, shaking breath. "I did it to myself."

Marilynn raised an eyebrow, and I braced myself for a harsh lecture. But instead, she patted me on the back like a small child. "Listen. It's okay. I know you want to help him, but maybe you just can't."

My eyes shot to Marilynn's face, stunned by her statement.

SEVEN

I DISCOVERED, IF needed, I could survive with only one arm...at least for a few days. Chores around the ranch were awkward, but I devised new techniques to complete them. My Olympic-discus-thrower method frightened the ranch horses a bit, but they stood still as I wrapped my good arm over the top of each saddle and used gravity to spin my body and launch the heavy piece of leather onto their backs. Thank God for obedient, trusting horses.

I also realized I could clean stalls by gripping the middle of the manure pick handle and using my armpit as a leverage point for the end of the long, wooden pole. I only placed my other hand on the handle, for appearances, when Marilynn was in sight. I don't think she noticed my newly devised stall cleaning technique. Either that or she was determined to ignore it.

Casey was more observant. He stopped in his tracks when I pulled a hay bale from the feed room and dragged it down the barn aisle by one strand of twine, leaving a trail of hay bits in my tracks.

"Need some help there?" he asked, forming his words slowly. "I can carry that for you...if you want."

"No, thank you," I replied, still dragging the bale and avoiding eye contact. "My left arm needs to get worked too. Been using my right arm too much lately."

I continued on in silence as if that was a normal response. Stopping at the end of the aisle, I cut open the bale, feeling Casey's eyes on my every move and awaiting his next question.

"Grab an extra bridle, Casey," Marilynn yelled from just outside the barn. "We're one short."

"Sure. Be there in a minute," Casey replied and turned to enter the tack room, keeping any sarcastic comments to himself.

I began feeding the horses, hoping Casey and Marilynn would head out on their trail ride soon. My next task was to dump a wheelbarrow full of manure. I hadn't quite figured out how I was going to accomplish that one yet.

I made it through the work day with no major mishaps or further injuries and my one-armed techniques seemed to give my shoulder some time to heal, to loosen up. Although, I knew I had to avoid the same situation tonight. My body wouldn't take kindly to another rodeo-bronc disaster. After a day of work, I realized how important each one of my limbs is and I didn't need to injure another one.

The arena was quiet this time. There was no one lingering around to judge Chance...or my dreaded cartwheels through the air. I took my time brushing his black coat and we relaxed together with each new stroke. Chance eventually cocked his back foot, resting the tip of his hoof on the ground, and took a slow breath, his lower lip hanging loose.

"Not so bad is it?" I smiled at him.

Convinced we were both ready to give it another shot, I grabbed the saddle and winced as I used both arms to lightly set it on his back. I knew Chance wouldn't stand for my Olympic-discus-thrower move.

Tightening the girth under his belly, I watched, horrified, as Chance transformed out of relaxation. Every muscle hardened as he planted all four feet on the ground. His black neck arched and his nostrils flared, showing the pink skin inside. The image was a replica of yesterday.

I jumped backwards, hoping to distance myself from the explosion, but Chance's stance didn't change. He just stood there, on the verge of destruction, and I racked my brain for my next move. *Maybe I should just let him buck...without me in the saddle.*

Moving with caution, I unclipped the lead rope from his halter and switched to a lunge line, a long cotton rope that would allow Chance to move in a large circle around me.

I stepped back again and clucked my tongue. "Just walk forward, Chance. That's all you need to do," I said, raising my free hand in the air. I should have flinched at my aching shoulder, but the adrenaline racing through my body seemed to mask the pain. And, just like yesterday, his frozen body broke into a blur. Only this time I watched the rodeo show from the ground.

Chance lurched forward into a series of rears, kicks, and snorts. He was stuck in his own world, blinded by fear, as he circled around me. And then, my gut flipped when Chance whipped his body towards the fence and I realized he didn't understand he was connected to anything...or anyone.

I should have let go, but I didn't and my whole body jerked forward with him. I found myself yanked into a run, my feet grazing the dirt every ten feet or so. I was nearly flying before the lunge line ripped from my hand and I tripped over my own feet, rolling and then skidding to a stop on my butt. Reunited with the arena dirt, I sat and watched as Chance gallop around the arena with the lunge line dragging behind him.

I rested my head in my hands. *I don't think I'm doing anything good for him.*

"Chance giving you a hard time?"

I stopped breathing at the question and peeked through my fingers to find Casey, sitting on top of Rocky. How long had he been on the other side of the fence watching me? I wanted to dissolve into the ground, melt away, run back to my bunk. Having Casey watch me fail was a thousand times worse than having Taylor watch me fail.

Swallowing what was left of my pride, I stood up and brushed the dirt from my jeans. At least I didn't have to spit it out of my mouth this time. "I'm not sure what I'm doing wrong," I confessed.

Casey scrunched his eyebrows together, slouching to rest his forearms on the saddle horn. He was quiet, processing the situation. "I think you're on the right track," he noted. "It looks like Chance is too anxious to accept the saddle right now."

"Maybe a horse-sized Prozac would help," I said, rubbing my shoulder as Chance blazed another lap around the arena.

"Probably," Casey chuckled. "But I think you just need to get his mind in the right place."

"I was trying to do that," I sighed. "I took an hour to brush him and rub on him and I thought he was ready. Apparently, he wasn't." I shook my head.

"I think he needs a longer warm-up. He needs to work out his fears first. Then he'll be more accepting of the saddle...and a rider."

"Think about it this way," Casey continued. "A horse is a prey animal. His instinct is to protect himself from a predator...through fight or flight. Right now Chance is in flight mode. He's trying to run away from the scary saddle strapped to his back. You have to give him some time to realize that the saddle isn't going to hurt him." Casey nodded towards Chance. "Can I help?"

Casey was making sense, but I didn't want his charity. I wanted to do this on my own.

"Come on," Casey urged. "Before you hurt the other arm and you have to pull hay bales around with your feet." Casey's lips turned up at the corners and I rolled my eyes.

My two week trial period with Chance was getting shorter by the minute. I didn't have time to spare. "I guess," I said, giving in. "I'm not very handy with my feet."

Casey sat up in the saddle. "Okay then, let's see if we can round up Chance together."

Casey guided Rocky through the gate and I closed it behind him. The two rode out into the middle of the arena and Chance's running came to an abrupt stop. He whinnied at the top of his lungs and trotted across the arena in sharp strides. The lunge line had been snapped off and shortened during his outburst. It was now dangling from his halter, barely brushing the ground.

Chance approached the gray gelding and stiffed at his nose and neck. Rocky stood still, ignoring Chance and listening to Casey. And, while Chance was distracted, Casey grabbed what was left of the lunge line and wrapped it around Rocky's saddle horn. Chance didn't seem to notice until Casey asked Rocky to walk forward.

Chance baulked when the rope tightened and pulled at his halter, but Rocky continued walking and Chance was forced to follow. Casey moved both horses into a trot and quickly to a lope. And, loping, Chance wrenched his head down and jumped hard, making that awful guttural noise. I clenched my eyes shut, listening to the horses thunder around me. A few laps and the guttural noise stopped. I opened my eyes, searching the arena, and found Chance loping shoulder to shoulder with Rocky, following his speed.

Realizing my stubby nails were digging into the palms of my hands, I released my fingers and wiped the sweat on my jeans.

"You got him to stop bucking," I said, my mouth gapping open as Casey slowed the two horses to a walk in front of me.

"That was a start," Casey replied. "He needs more time before you can get on him, but I think he's accepted that the saddle isn't going anywhere. And that it isn't hurting him."

"Thank you…," I started, trying to find the appropriate words and wondering if Casey should be the one helping Chance.

"We're not done," Casey responded, cutting me off. "I think we should take him for a real ride. I was going to head into the mountain to check on the cattle yet tonight. Let's take Chance with. That will give him some more time to get used to the saddle."

"Okay." That sounded like a good plan. "I'll go get Sunny out of the pasture and saddle her up."

Casey stretched out his hand. "Hop on with me."

I almost fell backwards onto my butt again.

"Come on," Casey urged. "The sun will be down soon and it will take too long to saddle up Sunny."

Realizing my face was probably broadcasting my shock, I cleared my throat. Casey did have a point. We didn't have much time before daylight was gone. I managed a slow step towards Rocky and placed my foot in Casey's stirrup. I grabbed hold of Casey's hand and he pulled me up.

I landed behind his saddle and sat in silence for a few moments, not sure where to put my hands. Feeling rushed to make a decision, I gripped the cantle, the back of the saddle seat.

"You ready back there?" Casey turned his head and pushed his sandy brown hair from his eyes.

"Ready," I squeaked out, thinking I might feel more comfortable on Chance's back.

Casey gathered his reins, clucked to Rocky, and the four of us walked out of the arena toward the mountain.

EIGHT

MY HEART RATE hovered near a normal rate by the time we were deep in the woods, but I couldn't keep my fingers from fidgeting. I moved them in circles, rubbing the smooth leather of the saddle. I focused on Chance, his body next to my dangling leg, his head bobbing with each stride, and I searched for something to say. Silence felt strange being this close to another person.

"So, how'd you end up working at Red Rock?" I asked, hoping his story would fill the quiet, calm my nerves.

Casey paused and, for a second, I thought he didn't hear me.

"I can't stay away from horses," he responded.

I waited for Casey to continue, but he patted Rocky's thick gray neck instead. "Okay...Did you grow up here? In Three Rivers?" I prodded, not quite understanding his statement.

"Nope. Grew up on my Grandpa's cattle ranch in eastern Oregon." Casey's body swayed in the saddle, moving side to side with Rocky's easy rhythm. "My Grandpa bought me a pony when I was four. Crazy Alice. She hauled me all over that ranch. Kept up with the big horses."

Casey's words felt warm and genuine. Not a hint of his usual sarcasm. "Sounds like a perfect place to grow up," I noted.

"Yeah, my Grandpa and that pony taught me everything I know about horses."

"How'd you end up in Three Rivers then?" I asked, trying the next logical question.

Casey paused again and then cleared his throat. "My Grandpa passed when I was eleven."

The silence became ten-times more uncomfortable. "I'm sorry," I said in one quick breath, wishing I had chosen a safer question. "That's horrible." Now, I felt horrible. I opened my mouth and managed to remind Casey of a painful childhood memory. I should have asked him about the ranch horses, his favorite food, anything but that.

"I guess that didn't really answer your question though," Casey continued. "About how I ended up in Three Rivers."

"You don't have to tell me. I mean...I didn't mean to be so nosey." My apology came out a little bossy.

"It's okay. Might as well finish my story," he said, and I kept quiet while he continued.

"My parents couldn't afford to keep the ranch after Grandpa passed. We moved to Three Rivers when my Dad got a job at a friend's auto shop. I have to admit I was pretty angry with the world for a while. Thought I didn't want to see another horse for the rest of my life."

"I couldn't imagine my life without horses," I whispered and glanced at Chance. *Even crazy ones that make me eat dirt.*

"Well, turns out I can't either," Casey responded, leaning forward to smooth Rocky's mane. "My Mom took me to one of Red Rock's ranch sortings a month or so after we moved. Watching the horses brought back so many great memories and I knew my Grandpa wouldn't want me to give up on horses...on ranch life. After that, I started helping out at Red Rock after school and I was hooked again. The horses are what really saved me." Casey tipped his head to the side, peeking at me with the corner of his eye. "I guess that sounds kind of sappy."

"No, no," I said right away, shaking my head back and forth. "Not sappy at all." I understood. Horses could heal any ailment, any problem. It made total sense to me.

"So...are you ready to exercise these ponies?" Casey asked, shying away from the current subject.

"I'm ready," I replied, not sure what he had in

mind, but I wasn't asking any more questions at this point.

"You might have to hold on a little tighter then." And, Casey slanted his body forward in the saddle. At his cue, Rocky jumped into a lope. Chance raised his head, startled by the quick change in pace, but didn't hesitate to follow Rocky's lead.

Almost sliding off Rocky's rump, I grabbed for Casey, in instinct, and wrapped my arms around his chest. Before I could process what was happening, my body was pressed against his back and the wind whipped through my hair. Trees flew by our sides in a deep green blur as we headed up the mountain trail, suddenly intertwined.

I clasped tighter as we burst out into the open field and blazed a path through the middle of the cattle herd. With my arms wrapped around Casey's soft cotton t-shirt, it was impossible to ignore his solid frame. My face flushed hot, even in the cool wind.

The cows only watched as we thundered by, interrupting their evening peace.

As we approached flat ground, Casey sat back in the saddle, pushing against me. "Whoa, Rocky. Whoa, Chance." His words rolled out in an even tone.

The two horses slowed to a stop and halted on a cliff that seemed to overlook the world. The brown and white cattle dotted the field beneath us and, over the swaying tops of the fir trees, the ranch and the town looked miniature. The view went on and on until the ground blended into the peach and pink tones of the sky. I sighed from the bottom of my lungs.

"Beautiful, isn't it?" Casey said, taking in the scene as though he had never seen it before. I let every image soak in, not wanting to forget one detail. And, we sat there in silence. Only this time it didn't feel uncomfortable.

At least not until I realized I was still wrapped around Casey, my cheek resting against his shoulder. My stomach jumped and, not sure what to do, I sat straight up and yanked my arms back. Once again, I didn't know where to put my hands.

"You okay?" Casey turned towards me, his ice blue eyes meeting mine, his smooth skin bronzed from the afternoon sun.

"Just-taking-it-all-in," I said, my sentence blurring into one word. I felt like I should look away from his gaze, but I just couldn't.

Then Casey broke our eye contact, nodding towards Chance. "I think his mind is in the right place now."

I swallowed the knot in my throat and turned my attention to Chance. He stood with his head lowered next to Rocky's shoulder, relaxed. "He looks a lot different than he did in the arena."

"You should get on him."

I instantly pictured my face skidding across the hard ground. "Here?"

"Why not? Come on...I won't let you get hurt."

I stared at Casey again, blinking this time. And for some odd reason, I believed him. I nodded.

Casey directed the horses back down the embankment to the grassy field. He moved Rocky within inches of Chance's saddle and then Casey turned towards me.

"Swing around so both of your legs hang between Rocky and Chance," Casey instructed and I contorted my body to sit sideways on Rocky's rump, trying not to kick Casey or the horses in the process.

"And relax," Casey said, but I only stiffened as he slid an arm under mine, wrapping it around my back and clasping his fingers against my side. "Chance will only stay relaxed if you do...you have to stay calm for him."

And then I remembered what we were doing. And, I remembered I needed to concentrate on Chance.

"Put one foot in Chance's stirrup and I will help you get in the saddle. Even if he bucks, he's not going far. Rocky won't let that happen. I won't let that happen."

I took a deep breath, preparing myself for the unknown as I put the tip of my boot in the stirrup. And, before I could second-guess myself, Casey picked me up by my torso and set me in the saddle. As soon as my jeans touched the leather, I wrapped both hands around the saddle horn, waiting for Chance to explode underneath me, hoping Casey could hold on to him.

But Chance only lifted his head and took two quick steps to the side, balancing himself under the new weight. He didn't buck. He didn't run. Instead, Chance curled his neck around to assess me. He sniffed my boot with short, inquisitive breaths and, after an intense few minutes, licked his lips in acceptance.

I couldn't believe it. I was sitting on Chance's back. Sitting...not hanging on for my life.

Casey was grinning when I finally looked over at him. "Alright cowgirl, let's see what you can do," he said and clucked his tongue. Both horses responded to the cue and moved forward, beginning to trot. My body followed Chance's uneven strides as he zigzagged beside Rocky, unsure of my legs bouncing next to his ribs. I followed his every move until the zigzagging stopped and Chance moved forward with ease.

The cattle herd parted for us, creating a wide path through the grassy field and the horses took advantage of the space, surging into a lope. My hips rotated with Chance's rhythmic motion and my white knuckles began to regain their peach color as I loosened my grip on the saddle horn, my confidence increasing with each steady stride.

Then, I released one hand from the saddle horn, dropping my fingers by my thigh. Loping along on Chance, I felt free, suddenly safe. And, without thinking, I threw both arms out to my sides, like temporary wings. I tilted my head to the sky, letting the mountain air wrap around my whole body and fill my lungs.

I glanced over at Casey, still riding by my side, but now shaking his head and laughing. Without taking his eyes off me, he leaned forward and we broke into a gallop.

The horses made their way down the mountain in the dark, but even the night couldn't hide my smile. My first real ride on Chance was beyond perfect and the scene played over and over in my head. And, I couldn't deny that Casey helped to make it happen.

"Thanks for helping us take flight," I grinned, as we approached the barn.

"Any time," Casey laughed as he put a hand on my shoulder.

I leaned in to his touch, closing my eyes for a second, but my thoughts were broken by an irritated question.

"Going to check on the cattle, huh?" Taylor stood with her arms crossed and her shoulder resting against the barn. I didn't know how long she had been there.

"Hey Taylor," Casey said as he stopped both horses a few feet in front of her. "Yeah, Lucy was my helper tonight."

I slid down from Chance's saddle. "I bet you were," she mouthed the words to me with one eye brow cocked. I didn't know how to respond. *What exactly did she think I was doing with Casey on the mountain?*

"Casey was also helping me with Chance," I noted, feeling like I needed to explain our evening.

But, before Taylor could go on, Casey stepped down from Rocky's saddle and Taylor's face morphed to pure sweetness, placing her delicate hand on top of Casey's forearm.

"I was just stopping by the barn to see if you wanted to go get pizza with me in town? I figured you'd be pretty hungry by the time you got off the mountain." She batted her long, black eyelashes waiting for his answer.

"Sure, just let me take care of Rocky and I'll join you. Lu, you want to come too?"

Taylor's head snapped towards me. Obviously, Casey didn't notice her disgust.

"Thanks, but I don't like pizza," I blurted out and shifted my eyes away from Taylor's. I loved pizza, but it was the first excuse that came to my head. I certainly didn't want to be a third wheel. Especially when I felt like Taylor might push me out of a moving vehicle to get to Casey.

"Who doesn't like pizza?" Casey laughed. "You're a funny girl, Miss Lucy."

"Yeah, *super* funny," Taylor chimed in, cocking her head. "Maybe next time you can come with and we'll all hit up the burger joint."

It was clear Taylor's invite was not genuine.

"Yeah, we'll definitely have to do that," Casey said gathering Rocky's reins. "I'll see you tomorrow then, Lu. Have a good night."

"You too, Casey," I said, trying to ignore the possessive stares from the petite blonde standing next to him as she grabbed Casey's hand and directed him towards the barn.

"Sweet dreams, *Lu*," Taylor said looking over her shoulder.

I watched the couple walk down the barn aisle, hand in hand, and an unwanted twinge of jealousy physically gathered in my gut. I closed my eyes to erase the image and Chance bumped my back with his nose, knocking me back into reality.

"Sorry, boy." I turned. "I didn't mean to ignore you. You were amazing tonight." I rubbed the tiny white star on his forehead. "Now I know we can impress Mr. Owens if we just keep working at it. Hopefully he'll let the ranch be your new home." Chance sighed, lowering his head. "Let's get your saddle off and give you a well-deserved grooming. I think I even have a granola bar for you."

NINE

"LOOKING GOOD, LU," Casey said, climbing the boards to sit on top of the arena fence.

"Thanks," I said as Chance and I trotted past. "I've been spending every spare minute working with him."

"I can tell."

A smile crept across my face at the praise, but I kept long trotting Chance around the arena, focusing my attention back to him. This week I crawled out of bed an hour earlier, spending that extra time with Chance, in his stall, brushing and rubbing on him, gaining his trust. Then, after evening chores, I led Chance to the arena to ride, lunging him first to work out any anxieties. But, after a few days, Chance gave up on the bucking. In fact, I think he was starting to enjoy our time in the arena.

Leaning my body forward in the saddle, I made a kissing noise with my mouth, asking Chance to lope. Knowing he was supposed to speed up, he extended his trot, clipping along faster and faster. I balanced myself through the quick, choppy strides and kept encouraging him until he broke into a smooth lope, and together we moved steadily around the end of the arena. My heart swelled seeing his improvements.

As we started loping through the middle of the arena, I was so immersed in Chance that I didn't notice Taylor until Star was a few strides in front of Chance's nose. Realizing we were headed for a collision, I tightened the reins, pulling Chance into a small circle. Chance came to a jerky stop, shaking his head in objection to my sudden pull on the reins.

"Might want to spend some time working on his stopping skills," Taylor sneered as she posted in the saddle, not missing a beat and trotting back to the rail.

I growled under my breath. The only negative thing that came out of my evening on the mountain was that Taylor decided to put a target on my forehead. Instead of ignoring me, she was on a mission to keep tabs on me, to put me in my place. And, I wasn't a big fan of this new game.

Collecting my reins in my hands, I rubbed Chance's neck. "Sorry, boy. Didn't mean to yank on the bit. Let's try this one more time."

Accepting my apology, Chance trotted off. I kissed and squeezed my leg, asking for a lope again.

Chance extended his trot to the point that I had to concentrate on keeping my butt in the saddle seat, but I kept on him and he broke into a lope, following the reins as I guided him in a big circle.

"Nice job!" Casey shouted from the fence, clapping his hands together. Taylor wrinkled her face in disgust as she halted Star. I wasn't sure if the revulsion came from her opinion of my riding skills or from Casey's excitement.

Casey jumped off the fence as Chance and I slowed down to a walk. "You're doing a great job with him," he smiled.

"Thanks," I beamed, patting Chance on the rump, but my joy was short-lived as I caught a glimpse of Marilynn running down the path from the barn.

She waved her hands over her head to catch everyone's attention. "We have a problem," she shouted. Marilynn was out of breath as she crawled through the fence boards and jogged over. "I must not have latched the gate this afternoon when I left the quarantine paddock," she said, her panicked expression contrasting her usual confidence. "The heifers that Mr. Owens just bought from the cattle auction got out. I don't know where they are. They must have wandered out into the mountain."

"The heifers that the vet was just out to take a look at?" Casey asked, his eyes widening.

"Yes," Marilyn shouted and then slapped her thigh. "Ugh, I can't believe I did that!"

"What's wrong?" I asked. I didn't like the way Marilynn and Casey were responding to this.

"Other than the fact that we have ten heifers roaming the wilderness?" Marilynn put her hands on her hips, still breathing hard. "The vet is concerned they were exposed to IBR at the auction. A heifer purchased the same day is showing symptoms and the auction house called Mr. Owens last night to warn him." Marilynn shook her head.

"What is IBR?" I asked, my concern growing.

"Infectious Bovine Rhinotracheitis...IBR," Marilynn responded without taking a breath. I stared at her. That didn't help me at all.

Casey chimed in with an answer. "It's a viral respiratory disease and highly contagious in cattle. The vet didn't find any symptoms this morning, but it usually takes a week for symptoms to show up after they have been exposed. And, to make it worse, IBR generally causes miscarriages." Casey started towards the fence. "It would *not* be good if those heifers found the rest of the herd...the pregnant cows. We need to find them before that happens."

I pulled my foot out of the stirrup, throwing it over the saddle to dismount. "How can I help? Can I go get Rocky and Sunny for you guys?"

"No, the horses are at the far end of the pasture. It would take too much time to get them and saddled up. We need to be looking for those heifers now." Casey stopped, locking his eyes with mine. "We need you to help us with Chance."

I froze, one foot still in the stirrup. I had only been riding Chance for a week and I had yet to ride him out of the arena on my own. I had a feeling we would be more of a problem than a help.

Casey put a hand on the top board of the fence and launched himself over in one clean swoop. Marilynn slid her petite body through the bottom boards and they both looked back at me.

"Come on, we need you!" Marilynn yelled. "Casey and I will get the ATVs, but we need a horse to search the areas we can't get to."

They needed my help. There was no other choice, no time. What was I waiting for? I had to make this work. I tightened my grip on the reins and slid back into the saddle. "Get the ATVs and I'll start heading towards the mountain," I said, clucking to Chance.

Taylor loped Star past me before I could finish my sentence. "I can help too," she offered.

I didn't like the idea of having to spend more time with Taylor than necessary, but at least we'd have the help of another horse and rider.

"That'd be great, Taylor. We need all the help we can get," Casey said before he turned and sprinted with Marilynn.

I cued Chance into a trot and followed Taylor out of the arena. The ATVs buzzed in the distance as we made our way along the pasture's fencing, headed towards the thick timber. Taylor, in her English attire, had Star collected and loping along like we were on our way to the show ring. Did she hear Casey when he said we needed to search the *wilderness* for cattle? Did she think she was going to win a blue ribbon for this?

Chance's body was ridged. His head held high, unsure of the chaos. I tried to balance myself with his uneven, cautious strides, but I accidently bumped his belly with my heel. He pranced sideways, shaking his head in disapproval.

"Sorry, Chance," I whispered, gathering my reins and pushing him forward with a gentle squeeze of my legs. Responding, he extended his stride and, as we inched closer to Star, he began to settle, lowering his neck. Maybe it was a good thing Taylor was with us. The presence of another horse would keep Chance's mind at ease.

The ATV motors whined in spurts as their gears shifted, and soon they were on our tails. One right after the other, Casey and Marilynn whizzed by our sides and took over the path ahead. Star didn't seem bothered by the commotion, but Chance instantly felt like a grenade on the verge of bursting.

Resisting this new adventure, Chance lurched his head down and started hopping. I knew we were approaching bucking-bronco status so I braced my arms, keeping his head from getting too low. I would lose all control then. Leaning forward, I gave him a swift kick with my heels and it vaulted him out of his hopping episode. Chance loped a few quick, panicked strides and I clenched my fists as I tried, without success, to keep him from bouncing off of Star's hindquarters.

Jostled by our hit, Taylor whipped around and shot me a glare. "Think you can keep your beast under control back there?"

I really wasn't sure if I could, but Taylor's reference to "a beast" made me want to gallop up beside her and push her princess butt right out of the saddle.

"I'm going to do my best," I replied through gritted teeth.

"You think your best is good enough?" Taylor asked over her shoulder. Her words seemed to ricochet off the mountain as she extended Star's lope to catch up to the ATVs.

Chance chomped at the bit as Star pulled ahead and I tightened the reins to keep him from launching forward. "Come on, boy. Easy. Don't let her get to you," I whispered to Chance, but I was really talking to myself.

By the time we got to the edge of the woods, Marilynn was off her ATV and had discovered fresh, muddy tracks lining the old logging road that zigzagged up the mountain. "Casey and I are going to follow the logging road all the way up and see what we find. Hopefully, the heifers didn't veer far off the road," Marilynn said.

"And, hopefully, they didn't make it to the top of

the road," Casey added. "This road ends at the clearing on the far side of the field where the cows and calves are grazing."

"What can I do to help?" Taylor asked, directing her question at Casey as she tucked her blonde waves behind her ears.

"We need you and Lucy to stay together," Casey responded and I almost screamed. The thought of being alone with Taylor made my head hurt. "Slowly walk this road and see if you can spot the heifers in the trees. Marilynn and I will let you know if we find them further up."

"Here." Marilynn handed me a walkie talkie. "If you see anything, let me know."

"Of course," I said as Marilynn jumped back on her ATV and they sped off, leaving me alone with Taylor. Not exactly the person I wanted to go on my first cattle round-up with.

"Seriously?" Taylor asked, but she wasn't talking to anyone in particular. Star's reins were lying across her mane and Taylor had both hands on her cell phone. "My Facebook Ap doesn't work here."

My mouth dropped open. *Unbelievable.* Not really the time to be worried about updating your Facebook status.

Taylor rolled her eyes and stuffed her phone back in her vest pocket. "Okay, let's get this over with. It'll be dark soon and I am *not* looking for those stupid cows in the dark. I've got better things to do."

Taylor's only concern was herself, but she was partially right in her statement. There was no way we were going to find the heifers after the sun went down. We didn't bring flashlights or ropes or anything. We had about a half hour to find the small herd.

"Let's get going then," I said, guiding Chance to the left side of the logging road. Taylor and Star began to walk the right side and we both scanned the dense forest for signs of cattle. The horses kept a steady pace on the inclining road, their hooves marching in time. They didn't seem bothered by the tense silence. They made a better team than their riders did.

"You can't have Casey," Taylor said, out of nowhere. The words rolled sharp off her tongue, like little daggers.

"What are you talking about?" I asked as her eyes narrowed on me.

"Please," she said, pushing out one hard laugh. "I see the way you've been looking at him. Big puppy eyes, goofy smile. It's hilarious actually."

I diverted my eyes to the road ahead as my face flushed hot. I didn't know what to say. Maybe I did have a little crush on Casey, but I didn't know I was being so obvious about it.

"You know he's just helping you with that horse, right? Nothing else," Taylor said, digging her claws in deeper, making sure she left a mark. "Why would he be interested in you...when he has me?"

Each word slapped me across the face. I couldn't

believe how much they stung. I felt stupid. I wanted to turn Chance around and run back to the ranch. I wanted to sit in Chance's stall and wrap my arms around my knees and bury my face. I blinked my eyes to keep the tears from forming. "Well, you're wrong," I said without looking at Taylor. "I don't like Casey...not like that."

"Could have fooled me," she said, but then she shrugged and examined her french-tipped finger nails, bored by our conversation. "I hope they find those dang cows soon."

I wanted to find those cows just so I could get away from Taylor, but before I could grind over her words again, a deep, drawn out bellow boomed from the valley to my left. I walked Chance to the edge of the worn gravel road, following the sound.

"There they are," I said, looking down the hillside to a small band of heifers, mostly hidden by thick brush and trees. One chocolate colored heifer was staring at us. She must have been the one calling out.

"Holy crap," Taylor exclaimed. "We can't ride down that hill. It's too steep and there is too much brush. No way we can get to those cows."

I didn't care if Taylor followed me. *I hope she stays on the road and lets me do it myself.* Chance and I were going down there.

I pushed the talk button on my walkie talkie. "Marilynn? We found them. We are at the second switchback on the logging road."

The walkie talkie made a static noise and then Marilynn's voice came through. "Try to get behind them and start pushing them down the mountain towards the ranch. Casey and I will head back down and keep them from crossing the road. We are quite a ways from you, but we'll hurry."

I clucked to Chance and leaned back in my saddle as he stepped off the road and started down the steep embankment. Chance didn't hesitate at my request.

"Are you nuts?" Taylor asked, squeaking at the end of her question.

"No, but have fun hanging out on the road by yourself," I responded.

Chance took baby steps down the steep footing. Branches snapped under his hooves and tiny rocks dislodged and bounced their way down the hill. I leaned so far back that the saddle rested against the middle of my spine. I could hear Taylor grumbling in the background and I was thankful for every step Chance was taking away from her.

"Good job, boy. Easy does it," I said as Chance worked his way down the hill, thoughtful about every hoof placement. Even though we were moving down a near vertical slope, I felt safe in the saddle. Chance was taking care of me. I put slack in my reins and let Chance choose the safest path.

As we neared the bottom of the embankment, I watched the cows. The herd was still a few hundred feet away, but they were aware of our presence. They were starting to move, sticks snapping at their feet and calling to each other in warning of an intruder. My palms started sweating. The last thing I wanted to do was to scare the herd further up the valley.

But that is where they wanted to go. The herd started moving as one unit with their noses pointed uphill. They pushed through the brush and picked up speed. We needed to get in front of them. We needed to stop them.

Chance picked up his head, his ears pointed at the running herd. I tilted my body forward and Chance read my mind. He picked up a high-stepping trot and wasn't deterred by the thick brush. The herd was running alongside the creek and we trotted parallel to them, but the herd was picking up steam. We needed to get in front of them, to cut them off.

There was a clearing ahead, a short cut towards the creek and I gave Chance the reins, urging him to speed up, to cover more ground. He charged forward, but the trees had blocked my view of a major obstacle. I gasped when the fallen tree came into view. Its massive trunk covered the forest ground, stretching nearly to the creek. For a second, I thought about trying to jump it, but I knew it was too risky.

I tightened the reins to slow Chance, but he resisted, pushing forward against my grip. *This is where some stopping skills would come in handy.* There was only a stride between his chest and the fallen tree and I had no choice...but to go with him.

I leaned my body forward just as Chance launched himself into the air with a determined force. His knees tucked tight to his chest and my face hovered inches from his mane as we sailed over the tree trunk and landed on the other side. Chance didn't miss one beat as we glided back into stride.

Trees whizzed by as I crouched close to Chance's body, my head dodging hanging branches. We were now nose and nose with the lead cow and Chance dug in harder to push us ahead of the herd. As we neared the creek I sat back in the saddle, gripping the horn for balance. Chance skidded through the mud, coming to a sliding stop in front of the startled herd. I was shocked that I didn't end up in the water.

Chance stared at the chocolate lead cow, his sides heaving, and I caught a crazed look as it flashed through her eyes. I remembered how that young steer tackled me on my first day at the ranch. Only this time it was an entire herd of cows that wanted to get by me. My fingers gripped the saddle horn tighter, but Chance didn't move a muscle. And, after fully accessing the big black horse standing in her path, the chocolate cow turned and started to trot downhill. The herd followed her lead.

Adrenaline pumped through my veins as Chance picked up a trot to follow the herd along the creek. I couldn't believe it. We stopped them. We turned the whole herd around by ourselves.

In the distance, I heard voices and glanced to the

logging road to where both ATVs were parked. Marilynn and Casey were jumping up and down, hooting with their fists in the air. Taylor and Star were about twenty feet down the embankment. They had turned back towards the road.

My walkie talkie buzzed on my hip. "Nice moves, Lucy! You and that black horse just saved the day!" Marilynn said, her voice brimming with relief. "Keep them moving along the creek and we will be there to help you as soon as you push them out of the trees."

My heart pounded as my smile returned. "Did you hear that, Chance? We saved the day!"

TEN

"YOU SHOULD'VE SEEN us, Dad," I said, pressing my cell phone to my ear as I skipped along the dirt path. "Chance was amazing! It's like we really clicked out there on the mountain. He understood exactly what I needed him to do."

"That's fantastic, Lu. It sounds like Chance is really coming around."

"He is, Dad. He really is. We pushed the whole herd out of the woods on our own and then helped Marilynn and Casey guide them right back into the quarantine pasture. Chance did such a good job." My heart warmed remembering how Chance took care of me.

"It sounds like you're the one doing a good job with him, Lucy. Has Mr. Owens made his decision on the auction yet?"

"Not yet," I sighed. "But, Mr. Owens has got to let him stay on the ranch. I can't even imagine having to load Chance on a trailer and say goodbye to him now."

"Well, taking care of a horse is expensive. You know that, Lucy. I just don't want you to get your hopes up too high."

"I know, Dad." I understood what he was saying, but I couldn't accept it. Chance was improving every day and I just knew that Mr. Owens would notice his progress and see his potential as a ranch horse. "I'll try not to get my hopes up," I said, lying.

"Where are you off to now? It sounds like you're outside."

"Headed to the main lodge. Mr. Owens invited Marilyn, Casey, and I for a prime rib dinner as a thank you."

"Quite the thank you," Dad noted and then paused. "So, what is this Casey boy like? Do I have to worry about any hanky-panky going on while you are there?"

Hanky-panky? Who says that anymore? "No, Dad. Don't worry. We are just friends." I kicked the dirt as the words left my mouth and a few rocks bounced down the path. *I wish there was something he had to worry about.*

"I figured that, but I just wanted to make sure. Have a good dinner, honey, and call me tomorrow. Love you."

"Love you too," I said, stepping on the front deck of the main lodge. Guests swayed in a line of wooden rocking chairs and I smiled in greeting as I grabbed the handle of the double screen door.

Dinner was in full swing and the dining room bustled. The thick smell of comfort food filled my lungs and my stomach growled in response. Long rustic wood tables adorned with white candles and fresh wildflowers were fully occupied by guests. A gray stone fireplace separated the dining room from a cozy sitting area and everyone chatted as dinner was served, country music radio playing in the background.

I'd been in the lodge before, but never during dinner time. The ranch employees had their own kitchen next to the bunk houses and it was always well stocked. I had no reason to venture elsewhere, but I was excited for this congratulatory meal.

Scanning the dining room, I picked Marilynn and Casey from the crowd. They were sitting at the table closest to the fireplace, talking with Mr. Owens. And, as I started towards the table, I noticed another familiar face.

Across the room Taylor was poking her fork at her prime rib dinner, a look of complete boredom plastered on her face. The woman sitting across from her was, without a doubt, her Mom. The wavy blonde hair, tiny frame, and matching golden tans made the two look like sisters. Taylor's mom held a full glass of red wine in the air and tilted her head back in laughter.

The men sitting next to them looked smitten and Taylor's Mom was soaking up the attention.

Taylor sighed as she rolled her eyes and glanced around the room. Neither her Mom nor the men seemed to notice her misery and I hurried along before she laid her eyes on me. And, decided to let out her frustrations.

"Good Evening, young lady," Mr. Owens greeted as I took my seat next to Marilynn.

"Good Evening," I replied. "Sorry I'm a few minutes late. My Dad called."

"Did you tell him about your adventure last night?" Mr. Owens asked, shaking a few packets of sugar into his ice tea.

"Yes, sir," I responded.

Casey smiled from across the table and my heart fluttered for a beat. *I wish I could control that.* But, he did look handsome decked out in a baby blue starched button-down, the color matching his eyes.

"We were just telling Mr. Owens who found the cows and pushed them down the valley," Casey said.

"I didn't really do *that* much," I said, but realized they thought different as I looked at the faces around the table.

"Well, I appreciate having three reliable, knowledgeable ranch hands and I also appreciate hard work," Mr. Owens chimed in. "Marilyn and Casey were telling me how much time you have been spending with that black horse. Seems to me it's paying off."

I bit my lower lip, hoping he would say Chance could stay. "He's a really good horse, Mr. Owens. He's smart and athletic and he's a quick learner. It just took him awhile to figure out I wasn't there to hurt him. I know he will make a heck of a ranch horse." I could hear the pleading in my voice.

Mr. Owens turned to Casey. "You haven't heard anything from the sheriff's office?"

"No. No one has reported a lost horse."

"And, it's been almost two weeks," Marilyn added. "If someone wanted him, we would have heard it by now."

"I want him," I said. I meant for my statement to stay in my head, but it just blurted out.

Mr. Owens cracked a grin. "Okay then. The black horse has earned his place on the ranch."

I grabbed the edge of the bench to stop from falling out of my seat.

"He'll be your mount for the summer, Lucy," Mr. Owens instructed. "Ride him as much as possible and I'm convinced he'll be ranch-broke by the end of the summer."

"Oh, thank you, Mr. Owens." And, I meant it from the bottom of my heart. "You won't be disappointed."

"Good, now let's bring on this prime rib dinner," Mr. Owens said and motioned to the kitchen staff.

Nothing ever tasted so good.

I flicked on the barn lights and Chance nickered from his stall. His ebony neck stretched out over the door and his head bobbed in anticipation.

"Good morning. Are you ready for your breakfast?" I asked, walking down the aisle to the feed room.

Chance nickered with more enthusiasm as I dug into the grain bin for a scoopful of oats. I opened his stall door and Chance stepped back to let me in. His ears perked forward and he watched me dump the grain into his feed bucket.

I rolled my hand down Chance's neck, brushing his thick black mane aside as he nibbled on his grain.

"You get to stay here, Chance. Mr. Owens said you earned a place on the ranch." Happiness flooded my body as the words left my mouth. "You're safe here with me."

Chance's ears flicked back and forth as he lapped up the last few kernels of grain sticking to the bottom of the bucket. Finished, he sniffed the stall floor and then bumped my arm with his nose.

"No hay in your stall this morning, Chance," I said and rubbed my fingers across the star on his forehead. "Mr. Owens said you can go out in the pasture with the rest of the ranch horses." I slid the halter over his nose and clasped the buckle. "You ready for this?"

Chance stared at me, wondering why there was a

change in his morning routine, but he followed as I stepped out the stall door. His hooves clip-clopped on the barn floor and the other horses popped their heads over their stall doors as we passed through the barn aisle. They nickered and paced in their stalls, not approving of the change. In the last stall, Star flattened her ears against her neck, squealed, and pawed against her door with her front leg.

"Easy, ponies. I'll be right back to feed you."

Outside, Chance and I walked to the horses' pasture. The ranch horses gathered at the front fence, grazing and awaiting their morning grain. At the sight of Chance, Sharkie whipped up his head and whinnied a shrill greeting. Chance began to prance at the end of his lead and nickered a soft, unsure response. The rest of the horses turned to see what all the fuss was about as I opened the gate and led Chance in.

"You're part of the herd now," I said as I unclipped the lead from Chance's halter. He looked at me, frozen for a moment, and then turned on his haunches and galloped out into the field, bucking and prancing through the hazy morning fog.

Curious about the new-comer, Sharkie trotted in sharp strides to Chance. The two met nose to nose and sniffed until the pony pinned his ears and struck out with his front leg, shaking his head to show his dominance. Chance squealed and pranced away with his tail held high in the air and the little pony followed him around the pasture as Chance checked out his new surroundings.

After a few more introductions, the herd lost interest in the drama and went back to nibbling on the grass. However, Sharkie stood at the edge of the herd and kept a close eye on Chance as he romped around the field, sniffing and snorting.

I shut the gate and leaned on the fence, crossing my arms on the top board. He looked so free...so happy. Dancing around the field and weaving through the fog, he looked like he was meant to be there.

I sighed with relief.

ELEVEN

DESPITE THE HAPPINESS I found in my growing bond with Chance, my new joy couldn't take away the words Taylor threw at me on the mountain. Her harsh statements worked their way into my head and made me doubt myself...her words bothered me. *I wish I could say they didn't, but they did.* So I did the only thing I could think of to keep Taylor from attacking me again -- I started avoiding Casey. I figured Taylor would leave me alone if I left Casey alone. And, I wanted her to leave me alone.

Avoiding Casey wasn't an easy task as his bunk was next-door to mine and we worked together, but I gave it an honest effort. I had to avoid him. Lately, when Casey was near, my heart rate jumped and my mind flashed back to our ride in the mountain. I remembered my arms wrapped around his chest and my cheek pressed against his back. I thought about his soft cotton t-shirt and how he smelled like a combination of pine and vanilla. I couldn't push the thoughts out of my head. It was too much to deal with...so I just tried to *not* deal with it.

Instead, I poured my energy and time into Chance. Like before, I spent my evenings riding Chance, but I avoided the arena and the possibility of running into Casey or Taylor. I volunteered when Marilynn needed someone to check the fences for broken boards and hanging wire. Chance and I rode the fence lines, surrounded only by animals and nature and peace. My saddle bags filled with nails, pliers, and a hammer.

I wasn't a very good shot with the hammer so I was happy I didn't break any fingers, but the riding cleared my mind and strengthened Chance's body. In his short three weeks at the ranch, he was filling out, putting on weight and muscle. His black coat was starting to shine and there was a fresh gleam in his eyes.

"Good job today," I said as Chance trotted off to meet his new buddies in the pasture. Chance and I led our first trail ride today and I was so proud of him. He marched forward, leading the ride with confidence. The guests had a great time and even tipped me ten dollars. *I might have to go buy some more granola bars.*

I reopened the pasture gate for Marilyn and she led both Sunny and Sharkie through. She unclasped their halters and Sharkie loped across the field, straight to Chance. Chance nickered a soft welcome and nuzzled the pony's outstretched nose. Sharkie was miniature next to Chance's tall, lanky body. The chestnut pony looked like he could have been Chance's baby.

"He fits in well," Marilyn noted as we walked out of the pasture and shut the gate.

"He certainly does," I smiled. Marilyn's attitude towards Chance had flipped ever since our cattle-chasing adventure. I guess Chance proved his worth to Marilyn. I already knew his worth.

"Okay, so grab some lunch and then meet me in the arena at two o'clock. We are putting on a junior wrangler event this afternoon and we have twenty kids signed up."

"Junior wrangler event?" I asked, throwing Chance's halter over my shoulder. "Sounds fun. Do you need me to set anything up?"

"No, Casey and I have been setting up the arena all morning while you were leading the trail ride."

The mention of Casey's name altered my feelings toward the event. "Is Casey going to help too?"

Marilyn squinted one eye at me, trying to decipher my question. "Um...yes," she responded. "Did I mention we have twenty kids signed up? We are definitely going to need his help."

I guess I couldn't avoid Casey forever.

"There's a tray of cookies in the bunkhouse

kitchen," Marilyn instructed. "Can you grab that on your way to the arena?"

"Sure. I'll see you in a few hours," I said, thinking how I could dodge Casey at the junior wrangler event. I'm sure I could lose him in a mass of twenty kids.

Carrying a plastic tray stacked with chocolate chip cookies, I walked through the arena gate and scanned the mayhem. From the looks of it, I wasn't sure this group needed more sugar in their diet. A mob of small boys and girls, wearing plastic cowboy hats, bounced and weaved around their parents. Their high pitched voices echoed off the mountain as they shrieked with excitement.

Small pens were setup on one side of the arena and the make-shift petting zoo seemed to be a popular spot. A group of children fed handfuls of pellets to the five spotted ranch goats. The goats' actual purpose was to eat the overpopulating blackberry bushes in the pastures, but today they were basking in treats, hugs, and kisses from the kids.

In the next pen, a chocolate momma cow chewed her cud, unimpressed by the audience of screaming children, and her cream colored calf hopped and skipped around her in circles. A little girl with pigtails pulled at her mother's shirt, pointing at the calf's show.

A line of antsy kids stood next to the petting zoo, holding their parents' hands, and waiting for a pony ride. Tank, the big bay gelding, and Freckles, the leopard appaloosa, were the chosen veteran horses for this event.

Marilyn led Tank as he carried two red headed twin sisters through the crowd. He plodded along, not at all disturbed by the commotion.

"Put the cookies on a table," Marilynn said, pointing to the picnic tables in the middle of the arena. "And grab Freckles. She's tied to the fence, saddled and ready for the kids."

I nodded and headed towards the picnic tables. Mr. Owens was making rounds through the crowd, patting heads, handing out plastic cowboy hats, and chuckling like a jolly old man. The sight made me smile.

I stroked Freckles neck as I led her to the line of waiting kids.

"Looks like you're the next lucky girl," I said to the first kid in line.

The little girl's pink plastic cowboy hat jiggled on her head. She couldn't have been much over four years old, but she wasn't the least bit scared as her Dad picked her up and set her in Freckle's saddle.

"Ok, now I want you to hold onto the saddle horn and your Dad is going to walk beside you. Are you ready to ride Freckles?" The little girl bobbed her head and beamed as we started our walk.

Making our way to the opposite side of the arena, I couldn't help but to scan the crowd for Casey. And, it didn't take me long to spot him, surrounded by a group of attentive kids. He was showing the group how to toss a rope lasso in the air. A row of hay bales lined up behind him, each pinned with a plastic cow head. He was occupied with the roping lesson and I was thankful to be on pony-ride-duty. Maybe I *could* make it through the afternoon without running into Casey.

After multiple laps around the arena, all of the kids got their time in the saddle. Marilyn and I unsaddled Tank and Freckles and put them in the empty pen next to the momma cow and calf.

"Time for the stick horse races." Marilyn's voice boomed over the crowd as she handed me an armful of wooden broomsticks attached to stuffed horse heads. The yarn manes and miniature leather bridles sent the kids into a tizzy, jumping around me in circles, grabbing the stick horses from my hands. I was surprised to make it out of the kid-tornado unharmed.

"All junior wranglers must report to the obstacle course," Marilyn shouted and pointed to Mr. Owens who waved his hands in the air. The kids jumped on their stick horses and skipped, galloped, and whinnied to his side.

Casey was still giving his roping lesson and, with the rest of the kids occupied, I peeked over the shoulders of his audience. Parents snapped pictures as their determined, miniature wranglers flung ropes in the air. Giving a demonstration, Casey swung a wide lasso loop over his head and tossed it over a plastic cow head, effortlessly. The kids cheered and then tried to mimic his motions.

My heart melted watching his kind, patient actions with the kids, his big smile. And, in that instant, I remembered why I was trying to avoid him. I needed to focus on something else. Something that wouldn't turn me into a blubbering idiot.

As I turned towards the stick horse races, I heard one of the parents challenge Casey. "Let's see you rope something that moves. I think you've got that plastic cow head mastered," he chuckled.

The kids squealed in unison and pleaded with Casey. They wanted to see the real cowboy in action. As I walked away, I felt bad for the goats. It sounded like they were going to become part of the roping lesson today.

I walked on, but was baffled by the abrupt silence behind me. Peeking over my shoulder, I wondered what hushed the crowd and gasped as a flash of rope circle over my head and tighten around my chest. In a matter of seconds, I was roped, turned around, and facing Casey as he began pulling me towards him.

I had no choice but to walk back to him. All the attention was now on me and it would look bad if I yanked the rope off my chest, threw it to the ground, and ran away. So I played along instead. He reeled me in and the crowd clapped. Casey bowed and the kids jumped up and down, screaming for more. We locked eyes and I tried to contort my face into a state of annoyance, but I couldn't help it...I laughed instead.

"Now, you guys try it on each other," Casey said, still holding a gentle tension on the rope. And, the kids ran in circles trying to rope one another and giggling at their newfound game.

Casey stepped in closer to loosen the rope. He slid it over my head, the lasso rolling up my back, his blue eyes watching me. The combination made me shiver.

"Thanks for being such a good sport," he smiled, winding the rope back into his hands.

I grinned and brushed the dirt from my t-shirt. "That's me. Always a good sport." My response came out laced with sarcasm.

"I figured that was the best way to get your full attention," he said, pausing. I diverted my eyes to the running kids. "Have you been avoiding me lately?"

"No. What do you mean?" My words felt cold and full of lies. I knew exactly what he meant.

"You're being weird," Casey said, stepping in my line of vision, forcing eye contact. "Did I do something wrong?"

His forehead wrinkled and worry flashed through his eyes, making me feel guilty. Casey really didn't do anything wrong. *It's not his fault that Taylor attacked me. It's not his fault that I have some silly crush on him and he just sees me as his buddy.*

I sighed, grinding the toe of my boot into the arena dirt. "No, sorry. I've just been spending a lot of time with Chance. I'm not trying to avoid you or anything." I hoped the lie fooled him.

"Okay, well, we need to go for a ride again. I could use some company to go check on the cattle tonight. This time maybe you can give Rocky a break and ride your own horse up the mountain?" He smirked and tapped my arm with his fist.

How could I be mad at him? "Yeah, I can do that."

"Meet you at the barn around six?"

"I'll be there."

I was still torn about Casey, but I needed to deal with reality. He was my co-worker and he was dating Taylor. My crush would have to stay just that...a crush. At least I knew he enjoyed my company as a friend. And, I was excited to ride with him again. I couldn't wait to saddle-up Chance and race Rocky through the open mountain field. *I should bring a rope and see if Casey can show me a trick or two.*

"You're excited too. Aren't you?" I patted Chance's neck and he danced a little jig next to me as we walked. Looking ahead, I saw Casey swing open the barn door and jog in my direction. But his jog turned into a run and, as he got closer, I noticed the frantic look on his face. I had never seen him look anything but calm and collected. This new look scared me.

"Turn around," he said, waving his hands.

"Hurry, take Chance back to the pasture and..."

"What's wrong? What's going on?" I asked, not knowing what could be so bad that Casey would tell me to turn around and get out of here.

Casey didn't wait for me to process his statement. He grabbed Chance's lead from my hand and pulled his head away from me, trying to turn Chance around. He raised his free arm and clucked to Chance.

"Come on, Chance. Come on!" Casey begged, nearly yelling. But before Chance could react, Mr. Owens, a police officer, and a tall, scruffy man walked out of the open barn door.

The man paused and seemed to assess Chance before he pointed and shouted, "That's it. That's the horse that was stolen from my property."

I felt like the air had been knocked out of my lungs. I turned back to Casey and Chance. Casey stood motionless, still holding Chance's lead, and Chance morphed back into the scared horse we found roaming the mountain. He backed with frantic steps, pulling Casey with him. He reared, tossing his head back and forth, and jumped sideways in an effort to run. If I had been holding him, he would have ripped the lead from my hands, but Casey held tight. I wished he would let go.

"Easy, boy, easy," I pleaded. The white rim around Chance's eyes popped against his black skin.

"Yeah, that's definitely him. Crazy lunatic of a horse," the man grumbled and spat on the grass. A wad of chew jutted from his bottom lip and he wiped the brown splatter from his chin with the back of his hand. His skin was leathery and his shoulders broad, but he couldn't have been much over thirty.

"And you're obviously the rat who stole him," he said, pointing at Casey with his dirty fingernails.

Casey's jaw clenched tight, his eyes narrowed. His strong hands gripped Chance's lead until his knuckles flashed white. I thought he might charge at the man, but instead, he stood there, brewing.

"Now, now," Mr. Owens stepped in-between the two. "I won't have anyone making those kinds of accusations here. For one, your horse showed up here and we took him in. We contacted the police with the horse's information."

"And he showed up here skin and bones and scared to death," I shouted at the man and all heads snapped in my direction. "No one stole your horse. He obviously ran away from you. Could you blame him?" My heart was ready to beat out of my chest. I couldn't believe those words rolled off my tongue. I didn't know this man, but I saw how Chance was reacting to his presence and my gut told me to keep this person away. Far away.

Mr. Owen paused, staring at me, and I was afraid he was going to tell me to shut my mouth. Instead, he turned back to the man.

"Listen, no one here stole your horse. That I can guarantee. And how do I even know this horse is yours?"

"His registration papers are filed somewhere in my Dad's house along with all the other *horse crap* he accumulated over the years."

I cringed at his obvious distaste when he said the word "horse."

"Provide the papers and you can have him back," Mr. Owens said.

I couldn't believe it. Didn't Mr. Owens see how frightened Chance was? Chance didn't want to go with this man.

The man growled a few curse words and stomped off, headed to his rusty brown pickup truck. Slamming the door, he peeled out and gravel ricocheted off the barn.

A lump of tears balled up in my throat. Why was this man claiming Chance now? He didn't care about him. Someone who cared about him would have been searching for Chance right away.

I stepped towards Chance, his nostrils flared and head held high. Casey handed the lead rope back to me and gripped my hand. "I'm sorry. I was trying to warn you," he whispered. He looked about as stunned as I felt.

"It's not your fault," I said and rubbed my hand over Chance's forehead.

Gathering my thoughts, I turned my attention to the sheriff. "Who was that?"

The sheriff made a few notes and shoved his

small yellow notepad in his front shirt pocket. "Billy Jackson," he stated without emotion. "His Dad passed away earlier this year and left his estate to Billy. He lived a few miles outside of Three Rivers and apparently had a collection of horses, dogs, cats, sheep and chickens. Now the animals are Billy's. He came to the police station this morning claiming a stolen horse."

"But it took him three weeks to figure that out? Did he even know he was missing?" I asked, annoyed at the sheriff's calm demeanor.

"I'm not sure why it took him so long, but, if he can prove that is his horse, you'll have to give him back."

Turning to Mr. Owens, the sheriff continued. "I have your phone number and I will notify you of further details. Have a good evening."

"Wait, what about the other animals at his place? What if they are in danger?" I asked. I had a gut feeling that the other animals on his property wanted to run away too.

"I will send an officer out tomorrow to assess their living situation." And with that, the sheriff turned and started back towards his squad car.

I didn't know what to say. The sheriff left Casey, Mr. Owens, and I circled around Chance and staring at each other, without answers.

"He can't take him. He can't have him back." I said, breaking the silence.

Mr. Owens shook his head. "I wish he could stay, but there's nothing we can do if Billy proves that Chance is his horse. We'll just have to wait and see what happens."

Wait and see? I couldn't just wait around hoping that angry man didn't come back and claim his *possession*. Chance deserved better than that. He deserved a happy home and a person who loves him.

"There isn't anything we can do?" My heart pounded hard in my chest. I thought about pulling Chance's halter off and letting him run back to the mountain.

Chance's brown eyes blinked at me. He must have been wondering what made me so upset. He trusted me now. I couldn't break that trust and send him back to a place he hated. What could I do to make sure that didn't happen? What did Billy want?

"Money," I shouted out as quickly as the thought entered my mind. "It's obvious that Billy doesn't really care about Chance. Maybe he'll care about money? I'll scrape together every penny I've got."

The look of concern didn't leave Mr. Owens' face. Didn't he hear me?

"Listen, don't get your hopes up, but I will bring that option up if Billy follows through with registration papers and still wants him back." Mr. Owens sighed. "But there's nothing we can do until we hear back from him."

TWELVE

I COULDN'T FORCE myself to sleep. I squeezed my eye lids shut, but that only produced visions of losing Chance. I laid in my bed, wide awake, and thought of ways to pull together the cash to buy Chance from that man. I had five hundred dollars in my savings account and I could talk to my Dad about selling my saddle. I think I could come up with fifteen hundred dollars. *I hope that is enough to make Billy Jackson go away.*

Chance was happy at Red Rock Ranch. His whole attitude had changed in the few weeks since Casey and I stumbled upon him. He went from a snorting, striking, fearful creature to a trusting, playful, eager partner. I knew all of those wonderful traits would be lost if Billy took him back.

I asked Marilyn and Casey to lead the trail rides that next day. I wanted to stay close to the barn in hopes of an update from Mr. Owens, but, so far, there was no news. After my evening ride on Chance, I kissed him square on his whiskered muzzle before he pranced through the pasture to join his herd. The sun was setting behind the mountain and my body was feeling the effects of a few hours of sleep. I needed a hot shower and my pajamas.

As I grasped my fingers around my bunk door's metal handle, I saw Mr. Owens walking down the dirt path. I strained to read his body language as he walked towards me, but dusk made it hard to tell if he had good news or bad news or no news.

"Hey, Lucy. I was hoping I'd catch you before you got tucked in for the night."

"Were you able to talk to the sheriff today?" I asked, but the deep creases in his forehead became clear. I clasped the handle of the door, bracing myself for his news.

"Yes, the sheriff called about an hour ago. They sent an officer by Billy's house to check on the other animals. Apparently, the house and the barn are empty. Billy said he sold all the horses and various critters and Chance is the only one left, simply because he couldn't get near him without getting trampled." Mr. Owens grimaced. "And he wants him back."

I couldn't breathe. The sky was caving in on my shoulders, crushing me to the ground.

Mr. Owens continued. "He gave the officer his registration papers and the pictures on the papers

123

match Chance's star and left front sock. Chance is his horse."

I gripped the metal door handle until the inside of my palm throbbed. "Did you tell the sheriff that I wanted to buy Chance from Billy? If he sold the other horses, he must be willing to sell Chance too." The words spilled out of my mouth.

"I did, kid," Mr. Owens said, but the long pause between his words unsettled my stomach. "He wants five thousand dollars. Claims his bloodlines are worth it."

"He wants how much?" I felt like puking. "He wants five thousand dollars for a horse he hates and he couldn't even get near without getting trampled?" I couldn't believe what I was hearing. I didn't have five thousand dollars and there was no way I could come up with that kind of money.

"I'm sorry, Lucy. I wish I had better news. I even offered three thousand, but he's not willing to negotiate and I can't be spending that kind of money when I have twenty other horses to feed and a business to run. He's coming to pick up Chance tomorrow morning."

My mouth hung open. I was processing Mr. Owen's words, but I couldn't understand them. All I heard was that I was going to lose Chance and that I couldn't stop it from happening. I couldn't keep him safe with me.

"I'm sorry, kid," Mr. Owens said, scratching his

head as he turned and walked away.

The air felt like a thick fog as I stumbled through the door and into my bunk. I crawled onto my bed and curled into a tiny ball, pulling my pillow to my chest, trying to get some comfort. Silent tears rolled over my cheeks. I was helpless. I couldn't stop Chance from going back to Billy. I couldn't keep him here on the ranch with me. I was going to have to say goodbye.

Why would this wonderful horse come into my life just so he could be ripped away? What a cruel game for God to play...for me and for Chance. I pictured Chance being pulled into a trailer tomorrow morning, frantic and scared, and having to watch. I could already see the fear in his eyes. He would wonder why I wasn't helping him, why I wasn't there for him. The images pierced through my head and I slammed my eyes shut, grasping my pillow tight to my chest.

I couldn't let that happen. I had to run away with him. No one was going to help me save Chance and I had no choice. I didn't know where I would take him, but we had to get out of here...before tomorrow morning.

My revelation jolted me out of bed and I skidded across the floor. Pulling on my hooded sweatshirt, I loaded the front pocket with granola bars and stuffed my cell phone in my jeans. My bunk door squealed as I threw it open and it rattled shut as I rushed into the cold dark. The last thing I expected was to run into a solid, warm body.

Casey. He was standing on my front stairs and I slammed into his chest, catching myself on the wooden railing.

"Are you okay?" Casey asked, grabbing me by my shoulders. I stared at him, his warm eyes swimming with worry. "I didn't mean to scare you."

"It's okay," I mumbled, but I knew that nothing was okay. I stood frozen in his grip.

"I was with Mr. Owens when he got the call from the sheriff. I heard the news," he said, his grip holding me in place.

My lower lip quivered. I looked to the sky, trying to stop the tears, but Casey's compassion made it impossible. The tears stung as they rolled out of my eyes and across my lips. I could taste the salt as Casey pulled me in and wrapped his arms tight around my shoulders. I buried my face in his chest and my body shook.

Casey pressed me hard to his chest and, any other time, I would have felt safe there. But, I knew he couldn't fix this for me. I swallowed hard and raised my head from his chest. Casey loosened his grasp on me, but didn't let go. Instead, he tipped his head down to meet my eyes. His lips placed only inches from mine. For a few quiet moments, all I focused on was his ice blue eyes and his warm breath on my face. I could feel both our hearts beating.

"I have an idea," he whispered.

I stood there leaning on his support, waiting to hear his idea.

"I want you to be my partner in The Three Rivers Cowboy Race."

I blinked the tears from my eyes, wondering what he was talking about.

"The what?" I asked.

I was standing on my front stairs, pressed against Casey's body, inches from his lips, and about to lose my horse. I wasn't making the connection. What did a race have to do with any of this?

"The Three Rivers Cowboy Race," Casey repeated as he loosened his arms and let his hands slide back to my shoulders. The cool air blew between us and I shivered, standing on my own two feet again. "It's a race, by horseback, through Mount Hood." His eyes read my face with each word. "Teams of two have to complete a ten mile course filled with obstacles. And the first team to cross the finish line wins...and I don't have a partner."

I wiped my cheeks with the sleeves of my sweatshirt. I was shocked that Casey wanted me to be his partner for this race, but, honestly, I had a bigger issue to worry about at the moment.

Casey continued. "Did I mention the winning team gets five thousand dollars?"

"What?" My response came out as a squeak as I tried to swallow the lump in my throat.

"You could keep Chance if we won."

I repeated his words in my head. My bottom lip shook again and I didn't know if I was delirious from the crying or dazed from being so close to Casey, but I started nodding my head.

"Yes...yes." I nodded over and over. "Yes. Chance and I will be your partners."

The ends of Casey's lips curled up in a smile. "Okay, then. Why don't you try to get some sleep now. I'll meet you at the barn at sunrise and we'll wait for Billy. We're going to have to convince him to wait the two weeks until the race and then he can have his money." Casey rubbed my arms and leaned in like he had a secret for me. "Oh yeah, and we're going to have to *win* that race."

Gravel crunched and the breaks on the brown pickup truck squealed as it came to a sharp stop next to the barn. Attached to the pickup's bumper was a one-horse trailer covered in rust and green mildew. My skin crawled as the door slammed shut and Billy shuffled out.

His baseball hat was pulled down to his eyebrows and dark curls covered the back of his neck. Sweat and dirt had deepened the brim of his hat's red fabric to a coffee color. A rope hung loosely on his shoulder and his leather work boots kicked up dust as he marched towards me. I stood in the barn doorway, wondering what made him so mad at the world.

Chance was in his stall, finishing a few flakes of hay. At sunrise, I brought him in, brushed his shiny black coat, and told him I wouldn't let him go. His ears flicked back and forth, listening to my whispers. Chance didn't have a clue what this morning would bring, but he was content to absorb my attention, my love.

"Where's my horse?" Billy said, walking past me into the barn.

I glanced down at the pasture, but didn't see a sign of Casey or Marilynn. They were feeding the horses, but should be back any minute. *I wish they would hurry.*

"I want to talk to you about something, Mr. Jackson," I blurted out and jogged to his side.

"Unless you have five thousand dollars in your pocket, all I want is for you to point me to that horse."

"But I do...have the money."

Billy stopped mid-stride and rotated towards me. Square on, his intimidation increased. He reeked of gasoline and earth. "*You*...have five thousand dollars?"

My shoulders stiffened as Billy's dark eyes waited for an answer. I wanted to look away, but I didn't. "I mean, I'll have the money for you in two weeks. I'm going to enter Chance in the Three Rivers Cowboy Race and the prize money will be yours."

Hearing my voice, Chance poked his head over his stall door. Billy muttered a few choice words, waved me off like he was shooing a fly, and started walking towards Chance's stall. "I'm not waiting two weeks on some crazy scheme you have. You either have the cash or you don't. And, from the sounds of it, you don't," he growled.

Billy Jackson didn't give me a second look. He grabbed the rope off his shoulder and Chance's hooves scraped against the stall floor as he bolted into his paddock. My heart jumped into my throat as Billy threw the stall door open. *How could I stop him now? What could I do?*

I followed Billy inside the stall to witness Chance pacing against the paddock gate, trying to find an escape. I wanted to calm him, to comfort him, to save him from this man.

"You don't have to rope him," I shouted as Billy started to loop the lasso over his head, putting Chance in his sights. "I can catch him. I'll get him for you."

I needed to distract Billy so I could get to Chance and open the gate. At this point, my best option was to let Chance run.

But Billy didn't seem to hear a word I said. The lasso whizzed in circles over his head, picking up speed and threatening Chance with every loop. As Billy released the lasso, I reacted in instinct hurling my body in front of Billy to block the rope with my arms. I turned my face away as the stiff rope slapped my wrists, burning them. Frozen with my hands in the air, I opened my eyes to watch the rope hit the ground.

Billy cocked his head at me and his face flashed

red. "*Get*...Out of my way," he growled and pushed me to the side.

His force threw me to the ground and I bounced across the dirt, stopping only as my back cracked against the fence. The board's sharp edge jabbed me in the ribs, but I was too stunned to feel it. No one had ever pushed me like that. No one had ever touched me in anger. My eyes searched past Billy. I needed to find Casey or Mr. Owens or Marilynn. I scrambled to get my feet underneath me.

Dust still circling my body, I caught a blaze of black from the corner of my eye and I looked up to watch Chance flatten his ears, rear up, and strike out at Billy. His front hooves flashed just inches from Billy's face, knocking the coffee colored baseball hat from his head, sending it spinning through the air.

Greasy, dark curls exposed, Billy covered his head with his arms and tried, without success, to run backwards. Instead, his boot heel caught in his own rope and he toppled to the ground. His back thudded against the earth and air burst out of his lungs in a solid whooshing sound. For a split second, Billy laid still. Then his eyes caught mine just as Chance slapped his front feet to the ground, creating a solid barrier between Billy and I.

I didn't move a muscle, perched on my hands and knees, but Billy shot to his feet and scrambled over the fence. Chance snorted, spilling a heavy haze of snot through the air. In that same moment, Casey and

Marilynn ran up from the pasture.

Billy screamed obscenities, but he didn't look back. "Two weeks! You have two weeks with that lunatic!" Billy hollered. "I'll be here the night of the race. I don't expect that thing to win so you'd better find a way to come up with the cash!" He stomped off, waving his arms and shouting more insults.

Casey left Marilynn in the dust as he ran towards me. "Are you okay? What happened?" he yelled as he threw the paddock gate open. I looked at him, from the ground, and the confusion on his face turned to rage. With his hand still on the gate, Casey slammed it shut and turned in Billy's direction. He took five huge strides before I could stand up.

"NO...no, no!" I shouted after him and Casey slowed his pace, coming to a stop at the edge of the barn. "It's okay. I'm okay." *I think I'm okay.* Everything happened in a blur.

I pushed my hair from my face and stepped towards Chance. He was standing motionless with his head craned to the side, keeping his eyes on Billy. I laid my hand on his curled neck and we watched the truck and trailer pull out of sight, leaving only a cloud of dust in its tracks.

THIRTEEN

THE CANVAS COVERED wagon rolled out at the crack of dawn. The wooden wheels pointed towards the mountain as the ranch's two blonde Belgian draft mares, Ying and Yang, pulled it along at a steady pace. Casey and I packed the wagon to its brim with tents, sleeping bags, loaded coolers, and firewood before Ernie, the head cook, and Dusty, the ranch handy man, stepped on board. Ernie and Dusty occupied the wagon's front bench and waved as they started their trek up the old logging road.

The help of all twenty ranch horses was needed for the overnight trail ride. Mr. Owens and Casey led the ride and Marilynn and I followed behind, making sure the guests rode safely in-between. The day was spent navigating tight trails and shallow creeks, breathing in fresh air. Rocking back and forth in the saddle, the drama of yesterday melted from my head.

Strolling through a grassy clearing, the guests snapped picture after picture. Lilac and yellow wildflowers peppered the wispy grass field and tall, dark fir trees marked the edge of the forest. The rocky, snowcapped tip of Mount Hood stood proud overlooking it all.

My thoughts lost in the scenery, I didn't notice Marilynn until she moved Sunny within a few feet of Chance. "This is great endurance training for the race," she noted, her cheeks rosy in the warm Oregon sun.

Marilynn was quick to voice her doubts when Casey and I told her our plan for the race. And her doubts were valid. To be honest, I was skeptical of our plan, but I couldn't come up with a better way to make five thousand dollars in two weeks. We just had to make it work.

Marilynn rested her forearm on the saddle horn. "You and Casey have a lot of work to do in two short weeks," she said, pausing to raise an eyebrow. "You'll have to be ready for anything. The ride is tough...on you and on the horses. And they throw some crazy obstacles in the mix. Herding, jumping, whatever."

"I know," I said rolling my hand over Chance's black neck. "We have a lot of work to do. I'm just glad Casey is my partner. I couldn't ask for a better shot at winning."

"Yeah," Marilyn agreed. "Did you know Casey's Grandpa won the first Three Rivers Cowboy Race twenty years ago?"

My mouth dropped open.

"Casey's been training Rocky for this race since he started riding him. He didn't tell you that, did he?" Marilynn asked when I didn't respond.

"No." I shook my head. "He left that information out," I half-whispered. He was relying on me to win something so important to him? Surely, he could find a more experienced horse and rider to compete with. I didn't want to be the reason he lost.

"There's Diamond Lake." Marilynn pointed ahead, realizing I needed a distraction. "You're going to love it up here. Come on," she said as she clucked Sunny into a trot. I focused my eyes on the scene ahead and tried to forget the uncertain thoughts pulsing through my brain.

Ernie and Dusty had the camp ready for the crew. Five canvas tents sat in a half circle around a smoky campfire. The covered wagon was parked next to a weathered corral where Ying and Yang happily grazed. Their black leather harnesses hung from the fence posts. And, behind the tents, a crystal-clear lake reflected the white and silver tip of Mount Hood.

Trotting closer, the hearty smell of beef stew wafted through the air. A dutch oven hung over smoky coals and Marilynn's voice echoed over the crowd.

"Everyone, unsaddle your horse and lead them into the corral. It's dinner time!"

"You ready to relax, boy?" I asked, patting Chance's neck as we came to a stop. Dismounting, I couldn't help but notice Taylor and Star. I managed to avoid her sight for most of the afternoon as she was attached to Casey's hip at the front of the ride. It was easier on me if I didn't see them together.

Taylor swung her leg over Star's neck and sat side-saddle, watching while Casey untacked Rocky. Her skin-tight jeans were tucked into her tall, black leather boots, intricately stamped with red and silver flowers. A matching bandana was tied neatly around her neck and her golden curls were wrapped in a loose bun. I wondered how many suitcases she packed for her summer here on the ranch.

I should have turned away, but I watched, in self-torture, as Casey helped Taylor to the ground. She put her hands on his broad shoulders and pressed her body to his as she slid out of the saddle. As her toes hit the ground, Taylor locked eyes with me. Realizing I was watching, she smirked.

My stomach flipped and I turned away, leading Chance to the corral. I tried to erase the image of them together but it was burned into my mind. I understood Casey was hers. And not mine. She made that perfectly clear. There was no need to flaunt it in my face.

The cool evening air rolled over my bare arms as I pulled my grey sweatshirt from my saddle bags. After a hearty beef stew dinner, everyone gathered around the blazing campfire, sharing stories, laughing, and roasting marshmallows. I slid the cozy sweatshirt over my head and inhaled the sweet, earthy mountain air. *I could live up here.*

Heading back towards the campfire, I noticed a silent silhouette by the lake shore. Casey. He was sitting, legs dangling in the water, perched atop a fallen tree. I started towards him, and then stopped, looking over my shoulder for any sign of Taylor. Hearing Taylor's distinctive cackle echo from the campfire circle, I knew it was safe to approach Casey.

"No s'mores for you?" Casey jumped at my question, but he smiled when he turned to see me.

"Actually, I already ate three," he answered and scooted over on the log.

Grinning, I kicked off my boots and rolled up my jeans. I took a seat next to him and dipped my achy feet in the cool water, listening to the crackling fire and story-telling voices in the background. The yellow moon bounced its reflection off the black lake and lit Casey's perfect face.

I took a breath, knowing there was something I needed to ask. Something I needed to know. "So, Marilynn told me that your grandpa won the very first Cowboy Race. And, that you've been practicing for the race since you started training Rocky." I tapped my toes on the glassy surface of the lake, making ripples. "Is that true?"

Casey nodded his head, watching the water run

off my feet. "Yes," he responded.

"Listen, I don't want to be the one to keep you from winning this race...a race that means so much to you," I said, half-irritated at his casual response. "I can find another way to get the money for Chance."

Casey snapped his eyes up, his forehead wrinkled. Now he looked irritated. "What are you talking about, Lucy?"

"I'm sure you know of a more competitive rider." I paused, thinking about the words I was about to say. They hurt before they even came out. "Taylor could help you win."

Casey's face didn't move, but a spark flashed through his eyes. He sat there frozen and took his time coming up with an answer, but when he finally spoke his words rolled out low and even. "I don't want to win with Taylor," he said. "I want to win with you. I *want* to help you get the money for Chance. Is there something wrong with that?"

I tried to follow his logic, but I just couldn't. "I don't understand. Why wouldn't you want to ride with your girlfriend?"

This time Casey's mouth dropped open. He looked like he wanted to respond, but his words were stuck at the back of his throat. "You think Taylor is my girlfriend?" he blurted out.

I about fell out of my seat and into the shallow water. "Well, isn't she?"

Casey straightened his shoulders and stared out

over the lake. "I didn't know you thought that. A lot of things make sense now."

Did I really make an incorrect assumption here? I guess I never did *ask* Casey if Taylor was his girlfriend.

"I mean...you guys were at the dance together...she's always flirting with you...you're always flirting with her." The words toppled out of my mouth. I was babbling. Maybe those things weren't concrete evidence. I started to feel like I should shrink up into a tiny ball and roll away. Far away.

"We did go on a few dates..." Casey admitted, his voice trailing off.

"I'm sorry," I said, trying to make sense of our conversation. "I didn't mean to bring up an uncomfortable subject."

"No," he continued. "Please...let me finish. I was going to say...we went on a few dates, but that was before I got to know you."

What? Did Casey just say what I think he said? Does he mean what I think he means? Turning his body towards me, his blue eyes radiated in the moonlight making my body numb, from the toes up.

And then Casey leaned towards me.

In slow motion, Casey wrapped his hand around the back of my neck and laced his fingers through my hair. He pulled me in with a soft touch, but stopped just short of placing his lips on mine. I couldn't hear anything in the distance anymore. Casey's breathing and my heart pounding were the only sounds.

My eyes closed as he pressed his warm lips to mine. Time stopped and I placed my shaking hands on his chest. For a moment, wrapped in Casey's grip, I was lost in a world I didn't know existed.

And then it came. A shriek so shrill it broke our perfect kiss. Both of our heads whipped in the direction of the screech.

My eyes had a hard time focusing in the dark, but when they did, I gasped. Although I couldn't see her face, I recognized the tall black boots. Taylor's body was rigid, her hands balled up in tight fists against her sides. And I didn't have time to move before more bodies came spilling out of the tent circle.

"What's going on?" Mr. Owens shouted as he ran through the grass, frantically shining a flashlight towards Taylor. Instead, the light discovered Casey and me, still wrapped up in each other.

No one moved. Not Casey. Not me. Not anyone watching us. The silence was awful.

"Lucy. Casey. I'd like to have a talk with you," Mr. Owens said, clicking the flashlight off and turning back towards the tents. I was thankful for the darkness. "Now, please."

My eyes shifted to the ground. The silence was deafening as Mr. Owens stood in the tent's open doorway, arms crossed. His body made a tall, dark silhouette against the backdrop of the dying fire.

"Do I need to have a talk with you about boys?"

Mr. Owens asked. I could tell he was uncomfortable without looking at his face.

Oh my God. How embarrassing. "No, Mr. Owens."

"I realize you are sixteen," he continued. "And both you and Casey are good kids, but I don't want anything inappropriate going on while you are under my care for the summer."

Until tonight, I didn't even know Casey thought of me...inappropriately. I still couldn't comprehend that he kissed me.

"And I don't want to have to give your Dad a call."

Mr. Owens' comment shot me back to our discussion.

"You don't have to worry, sir. I promise I won't do anything inappropriate."

He paused. "I will take your word this time, but I'm keeping an eye on you two."

"Understood," I said as I sat down on my cot and watched Mr. Owens walk to the tent on the opposite side of the campfire. He was probably going to give Casey the same talk.

Crawling onto my cot, I pulled the flannel lined sleeping bag up to my chin and zipped the side. I should have felt bad for getting in trouble, but my blood was still pumping from Casey's kiss. The recent memory took over every thought in my head.

What the heck just happened? Casey likes me? More than

a friend? My heart fluttered at these new thoughts. I stared at the canvas tent ceiling, eyes wide open, wondering how I was going to fall asleep tonight.

Mr. Owens popped into the barn more than usual for the next few days, but he didn't mention anything further about the awkward scene on the mountain. I was thankful he avoided the subject.

"What are you practicing tonight?" Marilynn asked as she took a seat on the wooden tack box.

I had Chance cross-tied in the barn aisle and finished wrapping a tiny rubber band around the end of his braided forelock.

I patted him on the forehead. "Casey wants to work on roping with Chance and then we are going to long trot around the pastures. Build up more stamina for the race," I said as I ran my hand down Chance's slick, ebony neck.

"I watched you working those steers with Casey last night in the arena. Chance is a natural. You guys work well together."

"Thank you," I said, beaming with pride at Marilynn's support. Every day Chance was making progress and my heart swelled at how much effort he put into our riding. Chance was quite the partner.

"Well, good luck with the roping," Marilynn said as she hopped off the tack box and patted Chance on the rump. "I just walked by the arena. Taylor is down there riding."

I swallowed hard.

"Try not to make her scream again," Marilynn smirked. "Although, it was pretty funny."

My body stiffened in the saddle as Chance stepped onto the arena dirt. Taylor hadn't muttered a word to me since she stumbled upon *the kiss*. On the ride off the mountain, I caught her staring at me, over and over, and I was afraid darts would shoot out of her eyes.

The arena footing was freshly tilled and Star's hoof prints seemed to be the only tracks. Taylor was riding in her western saddle and it looked like she had a whole obstacle course set up. Orange cones, poles, barrels, and jumps were scattered across the arena.

Taylor trotted Star over a series of red and white striped poles and then moved her into a canter as they headed towards a line of hay bales, stacked two high.

"Eyes up," a woman barked from the middle of the arena. "Look at the jump ahead of you, not at the ground."

The woman pointed sharply at the hay bales and adjusted the white visor on her head as Star sailed over the jump.

"Again!" she yelled. Her long, blonde braid swayed back and forth as she crossed her arms and shook her head in disapproval.

It looked like a perfect jump to me. I kept Chance walking along the opposite side of the arena, hoping she wouldn't yell at me next. *That must be Taylor's trainer.*

Out of the corner of my eye, I saw Casey trotting Rocky into the arena. Even with Taylor's uncomfortable stares, I couldn't help but to smile at his arrival.

"Hey," Casey said without a glance towards the lesson on the other side of the arena.

"Hey," I blushed.

Casey and I hadn't really talked about our kiss on the mountain. We were more focused on the race right now...and not getting in trouble with Mr. Owens. But, I couldn't stop thinking about it.

"Are you ready to try roping with Chance?" He patted a coiled rope hung over his saddle horn. "You've got your swing down. Now we just need to teach Chance a thing or two about roping."

I nodded. "Chance and I are as ready as ever."

Chance and Rocky walked side by side towards the roping dummy – a plastic cow head attached to a hay bale. Lost in my own thoughts about Casey, I forgot about the loud lady in the middle of the arena.

"Are you guys going to rope right there?" she asked as though the arena wasn't big enough for the four of us.

Not waiting for a response, she sighed and turned to Taylor. "Let's take a break while they ride. Otherwise, they will be in your way after the hay bale jump. I have to return some client calls anyhow since I had to cancel a week's worth of riding lessons for this race."

Taylor nodded as she trotted to the middle of the arena and dismounted. The lady stomped out of the arena without another word or glance back, fumbling in her pocket for her cell phone.

I looked at Casey. *Did I hear her right? Did Taylor's trainer just mention something about the Cowboy Race?*

Star lowered her head and licked her lips in relaxation as Taylor loosened her saddle's cinch.

"That's Linda Green. Ten-time World Champion," Taylor stated while grabbing ahold of Star's reins. Standing in front of us, her perfectly plucked eyebrows scrunched up into a deep "V" and her eyes were cold and accusing. She stared directly at me without blinking.

Linda Green. I didn't even recognize her without a trophy in her hand. Images of her wins were plastered all over the pages of the horse magazines stacked on my bedroom floor. She was one of the few trainers that excelled in rodeo competitions and the jumping world. Although, I had also read that she didn't exactly play fair. She did anything to win.

"Linda Green is training you for the cowboy race? The Three Rivers Cowboy Race?"

Taylor's lips curled up in a dark smirk, and the sparkle returned to her eyes. "Yeah, I heard you two were partners in the race," she said, pausing for dramatics. "And I couldn't resist. Thought it would be fun."

"Fun?" The word blurted out of my mouth just as fast as it entered my head and my worried tone only fueled Taylor's delight. I didn't understand why it would make her happy to mess with my only way to save Chance.

"And one more thing," Taylor added. "Linda *is* training me for the race...but she is also my partner. See you guys at the starting line on Sunday."

Taylor turned on her polished heels and whistled a happy tune as she walked Star out of the arena.

The gate clattered shut and I stepped into the damp, cool pasture. The moon was just bright enough to create silhouettes of the sleepy horses. Gathered together, their heads hung low and relaxed, but one black shadow perked up at my entrance. Chance nickered and stepped out of the sleepy circle.

"Hi there, big boy," I said as Chance walked over. He nickered again and placed his whiskered lips in the palm of my outstretched hand. "Sorry, Chance. I didn't bring any treats tonight. My mind's been on other things."

I couldn't sleep. My stomach turned. There were three days before the race and that was not enough time. In three short days there was no way I could gain the experience that Taylor's team had. And, I couldn't think of anything worse than letting down both Chance and Casey.

"We've got a big day ahead of us on Sunday."

Chance's ears flicked forward and his big brown eyes blinked at me.I wrapped my arms around his neck, tears welling in my eyes as I thought of losing him. Chance stood perfectly still, listening to me sniffle, letting me hang from his body.

Pressing my face into his coarse mane, my heart ached to be even closer to him. Through the tears I wrapped a hand in Chance's mane, jumped once, and pulled myself onto his back. On top of him, I felt safe until I realized what I had done. I didn't have a halter on his head. No lead to hold on to. There was nothing to stop Chance from running.

But, instead of reacting in fear, Chance curled his neck to the side and nuzzled the tip of my boot. Then, without a second thought, he put his head to the ground and nibbled on the cool grass.

Letting out an overdue sigh, I scooted back and laid my chest across his warm body, my legs dangling at his sides. Closing my eyes, I listened to Chance chew and breathe steadily. My tears stopped and my body melted into his.

The past month played through my head.

"Do you remember the first time I got on your back?" I asked, twirling a piece of his mane in my fingers. "You made me eat dirt."

It wasn't funny then, but the thought now made me grin. I kissed his withers and placed my cheek against his slick coat.

"You really trust me now. Don't you, Chance?"

I couldn't believe the leaps and bounds we had made together. And, we needed to make one more very big leap.

FOURTEEN

OUR ENTRANCE REMINDED me of a parade. The Three Rivers High School band split the crowds of onlookers as they marched down Main Street. Batons spun, trumpets blared, drums crashed and I was glad we were further back in the line-up.

Twenty teams signed up for the Three Rivers Cowboy Race and each team rode in twos behind the band. As team thirteen, Rocky and Chance walked shoulder to shoulder. Their hooves clip clopped along the pavement. Rocky was solid and calm, walking through the cheering crowd like it was an everyday occurrence, but Chance was unsure of the loud, congested scenery.

I tightened my reins as Chance pranced, every muscle showing in his upright neck. "It's okay, Chance."

"We just have to make it a few more blocks and we will be out of this mess and close to the starting line," Casey tried to reassure me.

My knuckles turned white as my grip tightened further. I attempted to smile, but my face was stiff, just like the rest of my body. I couldn't force myself to relax and I knew Chance had picked up on my nerves. He needed me to be brave for the both of us.

Rubbing Chance's neck I moved him closer to Rocky, hoping Rocky's quiet composure would rub off on him, but I over-steered. Chance got a little too close and I bumped Casey's knee with my leg. At the jostle, Casey's ice blue eyes caught mine and he grabbed my shaking hand. The background noise muffled at his touch.

"We got this, Lucy. We got this," he said.

The certainty in his eyes was so strong. Maybe what I really needed was Casey's confidence to rub off on me.

Casey continued to hold my hand as we rode through the last few blocks of burgundy brick buildings and through the blinking lights of the carnival. Past the bustling crowd and carnival rides, the teams of two were lining up in the open field. Chance and Rocky trotted to the starting line, a long yellow ribbon strung between two wooden posts, and I was glad to be out of the claustrophobic side show.

Each horse held their nose just inches from the yellow ribbon, and the last team, Taylor and Linda, trotted into place. Taylor was still waving at the crowd behind her as though she just won a beauty pageant. I was surprised she didn't wear a tiara for the occasion.

A little boy skipped along the yellow ribbon handing out sealed white envelopes to each team as a gray-haired man, dressed like an actor in an old western movie, gave directions over a bullhorn.

"Ladies and gentleman, cowboys and cowgirls, the twentieth annual Three Rivers Cowboy Race will begin in five minutes."

The crowd filtered in and gathered behind the announcer, standing proud at the wooden post.

He directed the bullhorn at the teams. "You may now open your envelopes to find the race map as well as a description of the first obstacle."

Paper ripped violently as each team pulled out an intricate map of Mount Hood.

"There are four numbered obstacles marked on this map. You may make your own path to each obstacle, but must complete them in numerical order. There will be a race official located at each obstacle. When your team has successfully completed that obstacle, the official will hand you an envelope containing instructions for the following obstacle."

"Two of the obstacles are team obstacles and two are individual obstacles," the announcer continued. "The individual obstacles cannot be completed by the same team member. And the first team to come back and race across this same yellow line, will be the winners of the twentieth annual Three Rivers Cowboy Race and the five thousand dollar prize!"

The crowded roared and cackled with excitement.

"There is exactly one minute left on the clock and the race will begin at the sound of my gunshot. Good luck to all twenty teams!"

Casey and I examined the race map in our last minute, deciding on our path to the first obstacle.

"Obstacle number one is at the base of Fallen Creek," Casey said, pointing at the red "X" on the map. "That's not far past the edge of the woods. Follow me after the gunshot. What does the obstacle description say?" Casey asked as I pulled the obstacle card from the white envelope.

#1 - TEAM Obstacle
On the hidden side of Fallen Falls, numbered rocks await you.
Each team member must find your team's numbered rock and
present both rocks to the race official.

"The hidden side of Fallen Falls?" I asked and looked to Casey for an answer.

"Ten, Nine, Eight..." The crowd chanted the countdown and the whole line of horses began dancing, reacting to the tension in the air. I tightened my grip on the reins just as the gunshot sounded.

The horses exploded forward in one unit, breaking the yellow ribbon and launching into the open field, but the gunshot was too much for Chance.

Chance reared straight up, balancing on his hind legs. I threw my body against the saddle and stayed curled in that position, waiting for his front feet to hit the ground. It felt like an eternity, but when Chance came down, he planted his feet and stood there, stunned. For a few long seconds we watched the horses galloping out in front of us, including Rocky.

"Go, Chance, Go!" I screamed as I snapped back into the game. I leaned forward and Chance pushed off into a full gallop. He ran, his legs flying in every direction, towards Rocky.

I held my reins halfway up Chance's neck and gripped the saddle horn with my other hand, holding my body in a forward position. Casey peeked over his shoulder and slowed Rocky when he realized we weren't by his side.

"Sorry," I exclaimed, out of breath, when we caught up to Casey. I steadied Chance with my hands. "I don't think Chance has ever heard a gunshot before."

"We can make up the distance. Let's just get to the first obstacle," Casey said and both horses picked up their speed heading towards the forest.

The herd of riders entered the trees in different spots and Casey pointed to an opening further down. "That should put us closer to the base of the creek."

I followed his directions and, reaching the opening, we slowed the horses to a trot and filed into the dense brush. Chance stayed close to Rocky, trailing only a few feet behind on the narrow path. His ears flicked back and forth, scanning the new surroundings. His feet were light, ready to jump in any direction away from danger.

"Trust me, Chance. I wouldn't ask you to do anything that would put you at risk," I whispered, lacing my fingers through his mane as we followed Rocky up a steep embankment.

On top of the hill, the base of Fallen Creek lay out before us. The horses stopped and we accessed our first obstacle. The creek poured off gray slate stone into a cascading waterfall and crashed into a small lake. Riders lined up along the brushy edge of the water, coaxing their steeds to jump in.

We trotted over and, reaching the edge of the lake, I gave Chance an encouraging squeeze with my legs.

"Look, it's not that deep. You can see to the bottom," I said.

Chance pawed at the line between the sandy shore and the water and then took two tentative steps in. Casey walked Rocky in beside us. That was easier than I thought.

"Now we just need to get those rocks," Casey said. He nodded towards the waterfall and I understood what the card meant by "the hidden side of Fallen Falls." We had to ride *through* the cascading water.

Rocky and Chance waded through the knee-high

lake and the waterfall sprayed as we got close, mist rolling through the air. Droplets collected on the horses' manes.

"Just go for it. Don't let it intimidate you," Casey yelled over the sound of the crashing water. He motioned Rocky forward and, before I had time to protest, the waterfall engulfed both Casey and Rocky's bodies. They disappeared.

When Chance could no longer see Rocky, he screamed at the top of his lungs, questioning the monster in front of us. He stood frozen, muscles tight, staring at the waterfall that just ate his friend. And I questioned it too. I didn't know how we were going to do this, but we couldn't waste any more time. There were already more teams riding into the lake's edge.

I clucked to Chance and, to my complete surprise, he launched forward into the waterfall without a moment's hesitation. Following the jolt, I threw my head forward and the heavy water crashed on my shoulders, pulled down the leather brim of my hat, and ricocheted off of Chance. We soared through in one swift jump, landing on the other side of the falls where Casey was waiting for us. He smiled from ear to ear at our arrival. I was just happy we made it through alive.

Inside the cave, Rocky stood in a shallow pool of teal water protected by a room of slate stone. Sunshine streamed through the waterfall at our back and illuminated the stone. The only sound was the crashing water.

"I guess that's one way to do it," I said before Chance shook like a wet dog, sending my body into the same convulsions and shaking away some of my nerves.

I adjusting myself back into the saddle and Chance picked up a high-stepping gait, splashing through the teal pool with Rocky. We headed towards the back of the cave where numbered rocks were scattered on dry ground. Stopping Chance, I threw my leg over the saddle and jumped to the floor, searching for a rock marked with a thirteen.

Casey was on foot too. We fumbled through the rocks until we both shouted, in unison. "Got it!"

We held up our rocks, both marked with a thirteen, and jumped back in the saddle just as another team burst through the waterfall.

FIFTEEN

A RENEWED ENERGY surged through my body as we rode out of Fallen Falls and into the warm sun. I brushed the water from my bare arms and followed Casey onto shore. If we could do that, we could do anything. Thrilled with our triumph, I patted Chance on the rump as we approached the first race official.

"Congratulations," she said, exchanging our rocks for another envelope. "You are team number ten to complete this obstacle."

Team ten? My joy melted away with her words. We were in tenth place? We had some serious ground to make up. I turned Chance on his heels and loped off after Casey, ripping open the new envelope with my free hand.

"Obstacle number two looks like it's about half way between here and Diamond Lake," Casey shouted over his shoulder, holding the map in front of him. "Let's connect up with the old logging road. That's the easiest path up to the lake."

"Okay, I'm right behind you. I'll read the obstacle description while we ride." I pulled the card from the envelope and focused on the words through the bouncing.

#2 – INDIVIDUAL Obstacle
Rope, Pull & Race.
Pick one member from your team to rope a log, marked with a red X, and drag it past race official #2.

"It's an individual obstacle and it's roping," I said, stuffing the card in my jean pocket and extending Chance's trot to catch up to Rocky. "This one is all yours Casey."

"Are you sure you want me to do it?"

"Of course," I responded without hesitation. "I watched you rope and pull a wild horse out of the mountain. A log will be a piece of cake."

Casey grinned and nodded at Chance. "He's not so wild anymore, is he?"

The horses' hooves crunched against the gravel as they stepped onto the old logging road. We covered about a mile of rugged ground, but Rocky and Chance weren't even breathing hard. All of those evening rides were paying off.

I pushed the damp hat off my head and let it hang from my neck by the leather string. Beams of sunlight shot through the tree tops and warmed my cheeks.

"We've got to make it to the top of the logging road for the next obstacle," Casey noted.

I looked up the steep incline and my eyes followed the zigzagging road back and forth up the mountain. The road had to be a couple of miles long.

"We've got to make up some distance," I said, noticing a pack of riders on the highest part of the logging road.

"I know," Casey agreed. "But we have to be careful not to push the horses too hard. They're going to need energy for the other obstacles. We can't just gallop up this road."

"Well, let's go straight up then," I said. My idea made perfect sense to me. "What's the shortest distance between two points? A straight line."

Casey gave me a blank expression and then looked at the terrain between us and the top of the logging road. The road was ten times the distance of going straight up the mountain, but the road was smooth and flat and safe. The uphill land between the zig-zagging road was filled with brush and inclined at a 45 degree angle.

"We'll make up some serious ground and you know our horses can do it, Casey."

And with that, Casey was convinced. "Let's do it."

I steered Chance straight for the incline, leaning forward in the saddle and wrapping my fingers into Chance's mane.

"We got this, Chance," I encouraged him. His ears flicked back at my whisper and he understood his job. I kept my reins loose and trusted in Chance's choice of a path.

He dug deep into the loose dirt and pushed hard with his hind quarters, moving us up the mountain. His chest bulled through the brush. At each flat road crossing, Chance jumped into a trot shooting across the log road and then launched himself back into the steep brush. Rocks dislodged under his feet and I watched them bounce, roll, and crash down to the closest flat landing.

Rocky stayed just inches behind Chance and followed our every move. Hitting the last incline, Chance kicked into high gear and loped hard through the brush and loose ground, grunting with his strides, pushing us straight to the sky.

Bursting out onto the last stretch of flat road, Chance snorted and pranced sideways, not ready to stop. I eased him to a halt, rolling my hand down his damp neck and patting his shoulder.

"Easy, boy," I cooed.

"Nice work," Casey beamed as Rocky trotted towards us. "The next obstacle shouldn't be far ahead now."

Glancing over the edge of the road, I noted five

pairs of riders still working their way up the logging road. Our short cut just put us in fourth place.

I smiled. "Now we just have to catch the rest of them."

Chance extended his stride as we trotted off the old logging road and broke into a grassy field. In the clearing, two horses, attached to ten foot logs by tight ropes, were pushing forward, dragging their logs across the ground towards the obstacle's finishing line. Their partners cheered from horseback on the other side of the second race official.

I pointed Chance's nose towards the cheering teammates. "I'll be waiting for you at the finish line," I said, nodding at Casey with a grin on my face. "I'll be the one cheering the loudest."

Casey nodded back and I kissed to Chance. He picked up a lope, gliding across the grass, but nausea engulfed my body as we approached the other side of the field and I laid my eyes on Taylor. Suddenly, I wasn't in a hurry to find my spot among the awaiting riders.

Taylor looked straight ahead as we approached. She didn't acknowledge our existence, but Star sure did. The chestnut mare flattened her ears and flicked her tail as I lined Chance up next to her. I was certain she would've grabbed Chance with her teeth if we got an inch closer. Taylor grinned at her mare's unwelcoming attitude.

Avoiding the awkward silence, I focused my attention back on Casey. He had Rocky placed in front of the pile of logs marked with red spray paint and was looping his rope in wide circles over his head. In one succinct throw, the rope snapped around the end of the smallest log and Rocky backed to take out the rope's slack. Changing directions, Rocky spun towards us and loped off, yanking the log off the pile and bouncing it along the ground.

He headed straight towards the rider in the middle of the field, Linda Green and her stocky buckskin. Linda was halfway to the finishing line, but Rocky was flying across the grass, pulling the log with ease.

I didn't even realize I was hooting and hollering until Taylor broke my focus.

"What are you yelling for?" she hissed, staring at me through squinted eyes. "You know Casey can't win this for you. Don't you?" She might as well have spat in my face.

My mind raced with all of the nasty names I was going to call her, but instead, Casey's yell jerked my attention back to the race.

"Whoa, whoa," Casey repeated, trying to calm Rocky.

Rocky was side-by-side with the buckskin gelding when he lost it. He kicked out, narrowly missing the buckskin, and hopped to the side, whipping his head back and forth. I gasped watching Casey lurch through the air, his body following Rocky's jumps as he held on through the frantic bucking.

Reins tight, Casey pulled Rocky into a small circle and the bucking began to slow. His jumps soon turned into erratic prancing and snorting.

"That's too bad," Taylor said over her shoulder as she walked Star towards the finish line to meet Linda, but I was more concerned by Rocky's episode than her comment.

Come on, Rocky. Get it together.

Casey rubbed Rocky's tense, raised neck and whispered soothing words until Rocky eased back into the steady, brave horse that he was. As Linda trotted her buckskin across the finish line, Rocky started to pull his log again. Calmed and listening to Casey's cues, he trotted across the field. His head lowered, Rocky pushed his body forward and pulled the log across the finish line.

I loped Chance to Rocky's side as Casey took the next envelope from the race official. Casey's eyes had a sharp edge to them. He looked straight forward, concentrating on something I couldn't see, and didn't mutter a word as we rode off.

"Are you okay?" I asked. "What happened out there?"

Casey broke his stare and shook his head from side to side. "Linda slapped Rocky on the butt with the end of her reins when I came up on her side."

"Are you serious?" I yelled. "You could've been

thrown! You could've been hurt! What kind of person does that?"

Casey handed me the new envelope as we trotted up the dirt path. "Someone who would do anything to win."

Ripping open the envelope, all I could think about was getting back at Taylor and her shady trainer. Now I had one more motivation to cross the finish line first.

SIXTEEN

#3 – TEAM Obstacle
Sorting Skills.
Separate a brown steer from the herd and chase it into the corral.
Once your steer is corralled, you will receive the envelope for the
final obstacle.

"THOSE CLOUDS DON'T look good," I noted, glancing over my shoulder. The high noon sun was beating on my back, but the eastern sky had turned navy blue and the dark color was crawling our direction.

Casey scanned the changing scenery. "Let's just hope it holds off until we cross the finish line. We've got other things to worry about right now."

Ahead of us, a herd of at least fifty black and brown steers jostled back and forth along the edge of

Diamond Lake. Riders weaved through the herd in their attempts to round-up a brown steer.

All three front running teams were now in sight.

Casey nodded at the cattle ahead as we passed the empty corral. "Just like we practiced in the arena, okay?"

I nodded back, realizing this was not like the arena at all. We were over halfway to the end of the race and there was no room for a mistake. I steadied my breathing and tried to focus solely on the task at hand, but so many images thundered through my head. This was not simply a matter of winning. There was a great deal at stake here.

All six riders, including the cheaters, were immersed in the steers, breaking the herd up into several clusters along the water's edge.

"Let's hit up the far end," I said and pointed past the riders to a small group of steers broken from the herd. Rocky and Chance broke into a lope, gliding through the tall grass.

"Easy, boys," I said, slowing Chance to a walk as we approached the curious cattle.

On the edge of the group, a chocolate brown steer stopped chewing his cud. He stared at us, swishing his tail. Surrounded by black, he was the only brown steer on this side of the herd. He was our target.

Walking towards the steer, Casey and I positioned our horses on opposite sides of the animal. I knew my job was to block him from running out into the field and I had to turn him towards the corral. He couldn't get past me.

Every nerve in my body was on alert, ready to react to the slightest movement. Chance, ears pricked forward, stared with intent and we waited for Casey to dislodge the steer from his group.

With Casey closing in, the steer made a sudden decision to run. But just as quickly as the steer jumped sideways, Rocky took two huge strides forward and cut him off. And it was on.

The steer stopped in its tracks and spun in the opposite direction. Then he was running, tail in the air, directly towards me.

At my cue, Chance lurched forward. We dived towards the frantic steer, blocking him from running into the open field. I pressed my reins against Chance's neck and he turned hard, following the steer, sending chucks of ground flying through the air.

Casey and I were now racing on opposite sides of the steer as the chased animal ran at top speed. Reaching my hands up Chance's neck, I gave him the reins and leaned in. Chance surged into another gear and we caught up to the steer's shoulder, turning him in the direction of the corral.

Casey and I worked together, pushing the steer straight to the corral and through the open gate. Pulling our horses to a halt, dust billowed up through the air.

A howl rolled out of my lungs, but the heart-racing thrill was short-lived as I watched our steer trot over to a single brown steer standing next to the fence. Turning Chance around, I caught a glimpse of the winning team loping off across the field...the hind ends of a flaxen chestnut and a stocky buckskin.

I tightened my stomach muscles and balanced my body over the saddle, allowing Chance to maneuver down the rough terrain. He kept his head low, assessing each foot placement. There was no simple path to the final obstacle so, looking at the map, we decided to blaze our own trail straight down the mountain. It was the shortest distance, but not an easy ride.

We were both silent, concentrating on each step as the declining path was filled with loose footing, fallen trees and overgrown blackberry bushes. There was still no sign of Taylor or Linda. *I hope we chose the right path to catch up with them.*

"Can you read the obstacle card?" Casey asked over his shoulder as Rocky lifted his legs over a series of fallen logs. "I know the riding is rough, but it's not going to smooth out until we are close to the final obstacle. And you're going to need to know the instructions."

By default, the last obstacle would be an individual obstacle...and it was my turn. I pulled the envelope out of my pocket and ripped it open.

#4 – INDIVIDUAL Obstacle
Jump, Jump, Jump.
The second individual on your team will complete a three-jump course.
Follow the marked trail that begins at the old log cabin and ends at Willow's Creek, where your partner will be waiting for you.
Then it will be a race to the finish line!

"Well, what is it?" Casey asked when I didn't say a word.

"A jump course." I cringed as I remembered Taylor would be the one completing the obstacle for her team. Anxiety bubbled up my throat. "We have to beat Taylor and Linda to this obstacle. I'm going to need the extra time. Taylor is going to breeze through this one," I said without pausing between my words.

"Easy, Lu. The clearing isn't far ahead. We will get out of this brush and the jump course should be right in front of us. We're almost there."

Straight ahead, flat ground and lush green grass poked through the tree trunk gaps. And, a few hundred feet to our right, the back of a rustic wood cabin rose above the bushes.

Goosebumps covered my arms and a shiver rolled up my spine as we pushed through the last bit of brush and followed Rocky out of the trees.

"I don't see any hoof prints," Casey noted as the horses picked up a trot on the wide grassy path.

Did we beat Taylor and Linda to the last obstacle? Or were they so far ahead of us that we had no chance of catching them?

I cued Chance and he picked up a lope, bobbing his head in anticipation. Rocky followed and we made our way down the path. The horses' hooves thumped lightly on the soft ground and the rhythm gave me some comfort.

In front of the log cabin, two wooden signs hung from a knotty, tangled tree that created a fork in the path. The sign on the right had the words "Obstacle #3" engraved along with an arrow pointing towards a wide path. The second sign said "Team Partner – Follow to Willow's Creek" and pointed to a narrow, dirt path veering off to the left and down the embankment.

Casey locked eyes with me as our bodies rocked with the rhythm of the horses. "I'll see you at Willow's Creek." His eyes were intense as he tipped the brim of his hat. "You take care of Chance and Chance will take care of you. You guys can do this." And with that, Casey sat back in the saddle, tightened his reins, and slowed Rocky to make the sharp turn down the dirt path. He had so much faith in me. Now I had to have faith in myself.

I watched Casey disappear into the woods. Then I leaned forward and Chance extended his stride, whipping past the cabin. His ears flicked back and forth focusing between the path ahead and Rocky's abrupt disappearance. He let out a short, high pitched whinny, but didn't slow down.

"Don't worry, Chance. Rocky will be waiting for us at the creek. We just have to get there." I rubbed the middle of his sweaty neck with the palm of my hand. "It's just you and me right now," I whispered.

A few heavy drops of cold rain splattered onto my bare arms as the first jump came into view. A series of logs lay across the path, separated by a stride's distance. I centered my body in the saddle and tightened my reins just enough to make soft contact with Chance's bit. His body collected under mine as we closed in.

One stride. Two strides. I moved my hands up Chance's mane to give him slack in the reins. He bunched up his muscles, pushed off the ground with his hind legs, and glided over the single log. Following the landing, he took one smooth stride and then launched himself over the second jump, which was actually two trees laying side-by-side.

Realizing the third jump was three laying trees, I braced my body for the takeoff and held my breath as Chance jumped. I watched in awe as the brown tree bark blazed by underneath his belly.

Landing on the other side, Chance loped off with an extra pop to his stride. Obviously, he was proud of himself. And, I was too. I sucked in a lung full of cold air and blew it out, relaxing back into Chance's stride.

Trees spray-painted with red arrows marked the

direction of the path, but it would be difficult to veer off. The path was cut into the mountain and was surrounded by a steep incline on one side and a sharp drop-off on the other. Following the arrows, I slowed Chance to trot as we approached a sharp bend. We followed the declining turn, with careful steps, that led us to a lower path going in the opposite direction. A glimpse of the second jump was now visible, further down the trail.

And then I heard the unmistakable thundering of hooves behind me. I whipped my head back to watch Taylor ride Star around the steep bend like she was circling a barrel at a rodeo. Her golden ponytail flashed in the wind as Star dove forward into a gallop, headed straight for us.

Chance jumped, startled at the sound of grass ripping below Star's hooves, and the jump allowed just enough time for Taylor to make up precious ground. Alarmed, but listening to my every cue, Chance gathered himself and burst into a fluid gallop. Taylor was only a few horse lengths behind us. We needed to run with everything we had.

As we ran, the rain began falling harder, pelting me in the face. I wiped it from my eyes, blinking to focus on the upcoming jump. Two large trees made an "X" on the path. The middle of the crossed trees looked to be two feet high, but the height increased towards the edges of the cross. We had to hit the middle.

Streams of water trickled over Chance's neck washing the salty sweat away. Chance probably welcomed the cool shower, but I knew the grass was getting slick. Our speed was too fast. I needed to bring him back to a collected canter for this jump.

Out of the corner of my eye, I could see Taylor approaching. She wasn't letting up. Star was in a full blown run, ears pinned flat against her outstretched neck.

I wanted to gallop through the jump, but I knew I shouldn't do it. Chance could slip on the wet grass...and he trusted me to take care of him. He would do anything thing I asked him to. And, I wasn't going to let him get hurt.

"Easy, boy, easy," I said as I sat back slightly and slowed Chance's stride. It pained me to hear Star thudding up on Chance's side, but I couldn't fathom risking an injury.

Five strides from the jump, Star's shoulder was in line with Chance's. Her petite frame was lathered in foamy sweat and her nostrils flared. Taylor narrowed her eyes at me and I expected her to fly past me to the jump. Instead, she gathered her reins and slowed the lathered mare to match Chance's speed.

I gasped when I realized what Taylor was doing. She was pushing me out of the way. I couldn't make it to the middle of the jump with Star by my side. Taylor had Star positioned directly at the center of the crossed trees and I only had two choices. I could try to stop

Chance and risk slamming into the solid trees...or we could jump the higher section, which had to be four or five feet tall.

My initial reaction was to stop. I closed my hands around the reins, but Chance's body told me otherwise. His alert ears, raised neck, and forward stride radiated confidence. The height didn't seem to scare him and he had no intention of stopping. His confidence sealed my decision. I leaned forward and my body surged with his.

Directly next to one another, the petite chestnut mare and the bold black gelding tucked their front legs and launched over the trees. Chance grunted with his effort. In the air, Taylor glanced over and was eye level with the sole of my boot. I fantasized about giving her a swift kick, but resisted the urge.

Star landed first and Taylor cracked her on the butt with the end of her reins. At the snap, Star jumped into a gallop, swishing her tail in annoyance.

I braced myself for a hard landing, but Chance touched ground and rolled back into a canter with grace. He extended his stride again and we closed in on Taylor. She had a good five strides on us, but relief rushed through me as I watched her ride onto dry ground. Sunbeams kissed the grass ahead. We were riding out of the rain.

The splashing of Chance's hooves turned back to pounding against the dry ground. His long body stretched out like a Thoroughbred in the last quarter mile of a race and we were gaining on Taylor. My eyes looked between Chance's pricked ears and focused on the only thing that could keep Chance and I apart, Taylor.

SEVENTEEN

POSITIONED BEFORE A sharp curve in the path, the third jump looked like a beaver's dam, a pile of large sticks gathered into a mound. It was a few feet high, preceded by a murky puddle that covered the width of the path and stretched out a few strides before the jump.

Remembering the race map, I knew Willow's Creek was not far after that curve and I pictured Casey on the other side of the creek, anticipating my arrival. It had to be killing him to sit and wait, not knowing what was happening. I imagined his tense face morphing into a beaming smile as I rounded that corner and raced towards him. I wouldn't let Taylor's face be the first one he saw.

My body must have conveyed my desire because,

at that thought, Chance stretched out his stride farther. We inched our way along Star's side, passing her rump and then her flank. Suddenly, we were nose and nose once again.

But I didn't want that to last long. I wouldn't give Taylor another opportunity to cheat, to jeopardize our win and Chance's opportunity at a new life.

I kissed and asked Chance for more. And he gave it to me. I could feel each of Chance's hooves push off the ground as though they were my own feet. We pulled ahead of Star by a nose. Then by a neck.

In a matter of seconds, we were three strides in front of Taylor and only a hundred feet from the last jump. With our lead, I eased Chance off a full gallop before we plummeted through the water.

Even with the decreased speed, Chance's hooves splashed into the dark puddle, spraying lines of water through the air like a Jet Ski skipping across a glassy lake. I didn't look back, but heard another loud crack and a few inaudible, irate words as Chance gathered his legs and pushed us over the beaver dam, landing with a few feet to spare.

Joy surged through my body as we galloped away and I peeked back to examine our lead. But instead, I was met with the image of Star, bucking and grunting behind us, her head held low, reins flying through the air...and no Taylor.

Star had cleared the jump, but Taylor was nowhere to be seen. The chestnut mare, realizing she had dumped her rider, shook her head from side to side and bounced towards us kicking up her heels.

Sitting straight up, I pushed my heels down in the stirrups and pulled Chance to a choppy stop. He pranced, confused, as I turned him around and directed him back towards the jump we had just cleared. I wanted to leave Taylor in my tracks. I wanted to keep running...but I just couldn't. Not like this.

Star whizzed by us. Her nose pointed high in the air, snorting. I couldn't blame her for her retaliation, but I hoped Taylor was okay. What would I do if Taylor had a broken arm? A broken leg? What if she was unconscious? A fall at that speed could cause some serious damage.

I held my breath as I slowed Chance to a walk. We approached the jump and my frantic eyes searched past the mound of sticks...and landed on a very unhappy face. Taylor was sitting in the middle of the shallow, murky puddle. Her knees bent above the water and her arms wrapped around her shins. Seeing me, she pushed herself up to stand.

"What do you want?" she snapped.

Taylor was soaked from head to toe. Muddy water dripped from her once-pink polo shirt and her blonde hair was plastered to the sides of her face. Mascara ran down her defined cheekbones. I couldn't tell if she had been crying or if it was just the puddle water.

Realizing my mouth was hanging open, I snapped

it shut. "Are you okay?"

"What do you mean?" she shot back.

I thought my question was pretty clear, but I asked again. "Are. You. Okay?" I repeated.

But my question only warranted a stare and a lengthy pause. Something was simmering under that look.

"You turned around to see if I was okay?" Taylor asked. The doubt in her voice alarmed me. Why else would I turn around?

"Yeah, I saw Star bucking and I thought you were hurt. We were going pretty fast before we hit that jump."

Taylor blinked her eyes, her forehead wrinkled in question. "You really turned around to see if I was okay?" she asked again, tightening her crossed arms. "I wouldn't have stopped for you."

Well, that was quite honest. Even soaked in mud, the true Taylor shined through.

But, then I thought I saw Taylor's hazel eyes glass over. She looked away and cleared her throat.

"Thank you," she mumbled, staring at the puddle.

Her words nearly sounded sincere, but before I could process her bizarre reaction, the ground rumbled and we both whipped our heads in the direction of the sound. Two riders were galloping their way down the path, headed straight for us.

"I'm fine, I'm fine," Taylor shouted as she splashed through the water and onto dry ground. "Go, go! You have to win this race!"

Standing on the side of the puddle, waving her arms wildly for me to move, I saw a glimpse of Taylor that had not yet been visible to me. Maybe she wasn't such an evil person. Maybe.

But I could tackle that thought later. Right now I had a race to win. Knowing Taylor was okay, I turned Chance in the opposite direction and the cool wind whipped against my face as we pounded down the path again, headed towards the final turn.

From the look on Casey's face, it must have been a sight to see as Chance and I blew around the corner. Red cliff rocks on one side, thick green trees on the other, and two galloping horses on our tail. At our entrance, the worry melted off his face and he positioned Rocky with his butt towards us, ready to run.

Chance soared over the narrow creek like it was a raging river, matching my enthusiasm. Casey cued Rocky and gravel spit out beneath his hooves as he matched Chance's speed. We shot past Linda who was standing on the ground, grumbling and holding the reins of both her buckskin gelding and Star.

A team of two cowboys riding two huge sorrels scrambled to catch us. They hollered in the background as we galloped out of the woods and onto the open grassy field. Side by side, Chance and Rocky's sleek bodies bunched up and lengthened further and further with each stride until I was certain we couldn't go any faster. Their front hooves reached out past their outstretched noses.

Ahead of us, the town of Three Rivers jumped and shouted, gathered around both edges of the yellow finish line. The muffled voice of the announcer rattled in the distance as I turned my eyes to Casey.

Amidst a blurry background, Casey's crisp blue eyes twinkled. His black cowboy hat had blown off his head and was hanging by the leather string around his neck, exposing his sandy brown hair whipping in the wind. And, he was wildly laughing...exactly the way he laughed that evening in the mountain when I rode Chance for the first time.

I laced my fingers through Chance's ebony mane as we galloped across the finish line and I realized Chance was going to be okay. He was going to be mine. The thought overtook my whole being and I didn't even notice the mob of people screaming at our sides. All I could think about was everything I had gained from this Chance.

EIGHTEEN

CHANCE'S BLACK COAT glistened in the last bit of
the evening sun. He stood quiet in the wash rack,
resting his top lip against the wooden hitching post.
His eyes inched shut as I hosed his body down. I
sprayed his legs, moved to his shoulders, and finally
drenched his back. The cool liquid carried away the
salt, sweat and dirt earned throughout the race.

Then, using a rubber sweat scraper, I squeegeed
the excess water from his slick body and stood back,
admiring my pretty boy.

"Come on, Handsome," I cooed, untying his lead
and turning towards the pasture. Chance willingly
followed.

Sharkie nickered at the sight of his big buddy,
welcoming him back. Closing the gate behind us, I
unclasped Chance's halter and rolled my fingers along

his cheekbone before releasing him to his herd.

"You're home now, Chance. You're home," I repeated before planting a soft kiss on his warm, whiskered nose.

The calm in Chance's brown eyes told me he knew my words were true. He knew we had both found our place on the Red Rock Ranch.

And, the summer had only just begun.

***

ABOUT THE AUTHOR

Brittney Joy

Cowboy Boots or Muck Boots...always have been my shoe of choice. An animal lover to the core, my parents didn't know what they were signing up for when they put me in a summer horse camp at the age of ten. I was hooked.

Horses became my true passion. At twelve I started working at a local stable - cleaning stalls and leading trail rides. At thirteen my parents finally broke down and got me my first horse, Austie. She was a spunky bay Quarter Horse/Saddlebred cross with a perfect white heart on her forehead. I grew up on her back and I learned so much from her. And, when it came time to go to college, I packed her along too.

My family and I now live in our own little piece of heaven in the Oregon countryside. We stay busy taking care of our two horses, three cows, ten sheep, fifteen chickens, and one very naughty goat.

For more information on Brittney Joy, Red Rock Ranch and upcoming equine-adventures, please visit:

http://www.brittneyjoybooks.sqsp.com/

And, come say "hi" on Brittney Joy's Facebook page:

https://www.facebook.com/brittneyjoybooks

Happy Trails!
~Brittney Joy